Millbury Public Library

D0111702

Millbury Public Library

Millbury Public Library

The Secrets of Belltown

Case No. 1

A Belltown Mystery

By
T. M. Murphy

J. N. Townsend Publishing
Exeter, New Hampshire
2001

J
Murphy
T
8/02
c/w

Millbury Public Library

Copyright © 1996; 2001 by T. M. Murphy. All rights reserved.
Cover art copyright © 2001 by Mark Penta.

Logo design by Richard Fyler.
Author photo by Amy Hamilton.
Printed in Canada

Published by
   J. N. Townsend Publishing
   12 Greenleaf Drive
   Exeter, New Hampshire 03833
   800/333-9883
   www.jntownsendpublishing.com
   www.Belltownmysteries.com

Cataloging-in-Publication Data
Murphy, Ted, 1969-
    The secrets of Belltown / T. M. Murphy.
            p. cm.– (The Belltown mysteries ; no. 1)
    Summary: High school sophomore Orville is only inter-
ested in making it through the summer, but then he discovers
who is behind the brutal murder of a neighbor in his town on
Cape Cod.
[1. Cape Cod (Mass.)–Fiction. 2. Mystery and detective
stories.] I. Title.
PZ7.M9565 Se 2001   2001023775
[Fic]–dc21

ISBN: 1-880158-34-5

Acknowledgments

The most underrated job in the world is teaching. I want to thank all the great ones who taught me, and I would also like every teacher to know that your job is crucial. You do make a difference! Here are the ones who made a difference in my life and urged me to go for my dreams: Bobye Coyle, Barbara McDonald, Ethel Deloria, Joanne Holcomb, Anne Steele, Paul Cali, Louise Houle, Dianne Gregory, Cecil Tate, Richard Hughes, James F. Murphy, Jr., Margaret A. Murphy, John McAleer, and the late, Sister Margaret Gorman.

I want to thank all the young people who have written letters to me over the years telling me to keep writing the Belltown Mystery Series, and I want to especially thank Jeremy Townsend for reading those letters and believing not just in the series but in me! You're the best!

To The Murphy Family,

You make me the richest man in town!

Chapter One

MY NAME IS Orville Jacques. I bet there are only two other Orvilles known to man: the airplane guy and the popcorn guy, and we all know the popcorn guy doesn't help. I'm not a nerd. I don't get my thrills from the Periodic Table of the Elements, and I don't have a pocket-pencil protector and I don't even have allergies. So, how'd I get stuck with this name? My grandmother forced my parents to name me after my grandfather's stepbrother's half-brother, one of those crazy family-tree things. It was my grandmother's deathbed wish. She recovered right after I was born. They say it was a miracle. Yeah, right! Right after I was named, she got out of bed and played eighteen holes with the local women's club! OK, I have glasses and a lousy name, but I'm not a nerd. I'm a pretty decent second baseman with some pop in my bat. I also do theater in the fall to meet girls and because acting helps my business. I love watching detective-show reruns; I have them all on video. I even have my own detective agency. I'm like "Magnum, PI"—without the mustache, muscles, women, or car. I guess my agency has been lucky, because

I'm constantly finding myself in trouble. It all really began a few summers back, when I was sixteen.

I live in a town called Belltown. It's named that because the townies used to ring a huge bell when the whaling ships returned from a long trip. They still ring it on holidays and special occasions. My parents think the bell sounds beautiful—and they may be right—but not when the town crier rings it at five in the morning on the Fourth of July. It shook my bed that summer. I tried to get one more hour of sleep before I had to get up and deliver the newspapers, but no such luck. My Great Dane, Ophelia, decided to sing along to the "beautiful sound" of the bell. I was going through my Rocky phase, so I cracked three eggs, put them in a glass, and swallowed. I almost puked as they slid down my throat. I kept thinking, "This will make my arms bigger." Spinach hadn't done the trick when I was going through the Popeye stage, so why would this work? I don't know, but you do those kind of things when you're an insecure teenager with a pair of pipe cleaners for arms. I carried the papers into the house, and I wasn't psyched because the Fourth of July brought with it the expanded edition of the *Belltown News*. This meant lugging around extra-thick newspapers with the glossy food inserts that always fell out. I looked through the paper to see if the Red Sox had won. My eyes scanned and saw the words that Belltown was famous for—"Late Game." I wouldn't mind if the Sox were on the West Coast, the game was at Fenway, an hour and a half away. I heard a knock on the door and put down the paper.

"Hey, what's up? Did you read the paper yet?" asked my friend Mark.

"Keep it down, Mark, you're gonna wake my parents."

"If that bell didn't wake them, then they're dead. Did you see the paper?"

"Yeah. What's the big deal? The Sox played a late game."

"Don't you ever look at the headlines?" Mark barked at me as if he were an avid *Wall Street Journal* reader. I picked up the paper and read aloud:

> Man Escapes From Bayside Mental Hospital
>
> A man identified only as 'Walter' escaped from the Bayside Mental hospital at about 8:30 last night after he knocked out a guard and stole the guard's car. Walter is in his late fifties. He is six feet two and weighs about one-hundred-and-eighty pounds. He has gray hair, green eyes, and multiple scars on his back. He was last seen on foot after he crashed the stolen car into a tree. He is considered very dangerous.

I looked up from the paper at Mark, and we both said at the same time, "Awesome!"

Mark was my best friend. He was a summer kid. From the first day of summer until the last day we spent almost every waking moment together. We stacked all my papers in a pile and took them outside. It was getting onto six o'clock in the morning, and the sun was now making its entrance. Joe Clancy was across the street sitting on his steps. Joe was a thirteen-year-old Star Wars freak, who also summered in Belltown. From Memorial Day to Labor Day, Joe would wear one outfit-his Popsicle-stained Luke Skywalker shirt and blue corduroy shorts. Joe was sucking on a Creamsicle while thumbing through a Star Wars comic book.

"Joe, it's six in the morning, and you're eating a Popsicle!" said Mark.

"No, Jedi. It's a Creamsicle. It's really good—do you want some?"

"Nah. Hey, Joe, did you hear about the crazy guy who escaped from the loony bin?"

Joe hadn't heard, and since we were sixteen and he was thirteen, we had to have some fun with him. I told him that the man cut off boys' heads and ate their brains, like Hannibal Lecter. It was a mean thing to do, but, to Mark and me, Joe was like a little brother, and you're supposed to terrorize little brothers. It's a law or something like that.

"So, like, does he eat their brains raw, or does he fry them?" Joe asked nervously, wanting to know but at the same time not wanting to know.

"I would imagine it would depend what kind of mood he was in," I answered, egging him on.

"What kind of mood?"

"Yeah, ya know, sometimes you're in the mood for a cold chicken sandwich."

"Yeah," Joe said, puzzled.

"And sometimes you're in the mood for a hot chicken sandwich. This Walter guy probably eats brains that way."

I was trying not to laugh when Mark added, "He might prepare the brains like a Thanksgiving turkey. Eat as much as he can hot and then get out the Ziplock bags and make sandwiches for the next day."

Joe's mouth was open like a largemouth bass, and he took the bait like one, too. We felt kind of guilty, so we let him come along with us while I delivered the newspapers. I was showing Mark my route because he was going to take it over for me in a couple of days. I was starting a real job—parking lot attendant for the Island Princess. The Island Princess is a passenger boat that sails over to Martha's Vineyard. I was hired to work in the parking lot, but I wouldn't be able to move cars until I got my license. So, I was going to be as useful as a blind dentist. I didn't care, though. It sure beat the 6:00 AM. bike rides. We pedaled along, talking about Walter, trying to figure out where he could be hiding in town if, in fact, he was still in town. All through the day, Walter was the topic of our neighborhood.

Around 3:00, Mark and I played our daily Whiffle ball game in my backyard. Joe sat on the swing set and watched, sucking on yet another Creamsicle. We battled for about four scoreless innings until Mark unleashed on a hanging curveball and sent it over the fence to Miss Sherwin's yard.

Miss Sherwin was our neighborhood ghost. My mother used to go to the bank for her occasionally, so she was the only person who had seen Miss Sherwin in the flesh for the last thirteen years. My mom described her as a nice quiet woman, in her eighties, who lived alone. That description was too simple for young kids to swallow. So we had our own crazy beliefs. We didn't know much about her except that in her youth she was a vaudeville dancer who had suddenly lost her hearing. The story around town was she ran away to become a dancer, and her father tracked her down one night after a show. He tied her down and poured hot candle wax in her ears until her ear drums burst, while yelling at her, "Dance to the sounds of silence!" But there were many stories about Miss Sherwin. One story was that she had an illegitimate child. Some people believed that there was a treasure map somewhere in her house that her great-grandfather hid before he disappeared. All I know is that we tried to avoid her house as much as possible, but now and again one of us would get lucky and hit the ball into her yard. The pitcher was always the unlucky one, and on this day I was the pitcher.

"Go get it, Orville," Mark dared.

"Yeah, yeah, calm down, will you?"

"Oh, I'm calm," he laughed.

I took a deep breath and hopped the picket fence. I kept telling myself, "She's a deaf eighty-year-old lady. She's not going to chase me out of here." The ball was lying right near the cellar door. I lunged at the ball, grabbing a patch of grass with it. I was about to hop the fence when I felt someone watching me. I was like the typical stupid camper in a horror movie. Instead of running away, I looked up through the pantry window. Miss Sherwin's gray eyes stared right into mine. She looked like someone from another time period—like a person in a black-and-white picture—but she was there in color, in flesh and blood, and she was staring right at me. She waved her long bony finger as if to say, "Get out of my yard." It appeared as if there was blood in the corners of her mouth, but it could have been smeared lipstick. I wasn't going to look any closer because I was out of there. I leaped over the fence and kept running past Mark and Joe and out of my yard until I was safely up the street at the beach.

"What happened, Orville?" Mark asked.

"Did you see her? Did you see old lady Sherwin?" asked Joe.

"Oh, I saw her, all right."

"What's she look like?"

"She's gray."

"What do you mean, she's gray?" Joe asked impatiently.

"Just everything about her is gray. Her hair, her face, her clothes, her eyes, everything except for her . . ."

"What?"

"Her mouth. It looked like she had blood or something red at the corners of her mouth."

Joe snapped his fingers. "She's a vampire. I knew it!" he said.

"She's not a vampire. It's the middle of the day. Vampires sleep during the day. Go on, Orville," said Mark.

I looked up at Mark, wanting to tell him to act his age, that there are no vampires, but I realized I had just run two hundred yards from a harmless old lady.

"Well, there isn't much more to tell except that she did point her finger at me warning me to get out, or else."

"Wow! I bet she was trying to cast a spell on you or something."

"That's absolutely ridiculous, Joe. Why don't you grow up?"

As I said these words, I tried to convince myself that it was ridiculous. Yet there was something about old lady Sherwin I couldn't quite figure out. She made me run like a crazed buffalo, but was I really scared of what she looked like or the stories that were behind the vision? For the next couple of hours, Mark, Joe, and I hung out at the beach. Every day Mark spent hours bugging the female lifeguards. I always thought this was a waste of time because they were older than us and wouldn't give us mouth-to-mouth even if we were drowning. Today was different. I was not complaining. I was still pretty spooked after seeing the old lady and was content to hear Mark's lame lines.

That night, our neighborhood was buzzing with bottle rockets and firecrackers. Everyone got blankets and headed to the beach to watch the fireworks. Mark and Joe were setting off firecrackers near sappy, unsuspecting couples. It was pretty funny how they disrupted one couple's pub-lic display of affection. The boyfriend jerked his head and his girlfriend yelled, "You bit my lip!" Even the rent-a-cop had to chuckle as he confiscated their firecrackers. I didn't light any of mine because I wasn't in the mood for that kind of stuff, so I jammed them into my pocket. I kept thinking of old lady Sherwin. I had seen her face for only a second, but it froze in my mind. Was that really blood on her mouth, or did I let my imagination run away again? Was she warning me to get out of her yard or was she warning me about something else? The more I thought about it, the more I saw concern in her eyes instead of the evil I had imagined. What did she mean? The question stayed with me all night as I watched the hours crawl by on my clock.

The next morning Ophelia, barking at absolutely noth-ing, woke up the neighborhood. I brought the paper into the house. I skimmed the paper, focusing on the headlines: "Belltown Fireworks a Success; Angels Beat Red Sox Again, 9-1; Man Still On The Loose." The last article basically stated that Walter hadn't been caught; and he hadn't even been seen. I went through my Rocky ritual, and ducked outside and waited for Mark. Mark didn't show. Joe didn't show. So, I got on my bike and flew past the beach. As much as I hated delivering the papers, there was never a more tranquil feeling than watching the sun come up at the beach. But, let's face it, I'd sacrifice that feeling for a couple of more hours of sleep. I made my rounds and then dropped off the paper to my last customer, who happened to be my math teacher. I have a theory that if God created humans, then the devil created math teachers. If I'm right, then the devil certainly had his say when it came to Mr. Reasons. His name was a complete irony. Everything about him was unreasonable. He flunked ninety percent of the sophomores he had. I was one of those sophomores. He was in his regular position, sitting on his porch, pointing at his watch, as I approached.

"Mr. Jacques, you are fifteen minutes and twenty seconds behind schedule."

"It depends whose schedule you're going by, Mr. Reasons, yours or mine," I smiled.

"You should show more respect for your elders, Mr. Jacques. I bet you wouldn't be so quick with your tongue if your father knew about your behavior."

"You forget, Mr. Reasons, my dad is an English teacher. He calls you people the Ninja assassins. Have a nice day, now." I rode off before Mr. Reasons could get any more words or numbers in. At about 9:30 I headed to the beach. When I got to the beach, I found myself the center of attention. Joe had told everyone I had seen old lady Sherwin. I kind of got caught up in the attention and exaggerated a little bit, strictly for entertainment sake.

"Was it scary, Orville?" a soft voice asked.

I looked through the crowd of listeners and saw Maria Simpkins. I had been crazy about Maria for years. I think the first words I ever said were Maria Simpkins. She had long black hair and a smile that would charm your grandmother but at the same time make you sick—a good sick. I had that feeling now. She was talking to me. She was asking me, "Was it scary, Orville?" Why is it the people we like make us dizzy and sick and stutter, and the people we don't care about we can talk to all day? I managed to stutter, "Nah, Maria."

"You're so brave!" exclaimed Mary Joyce, a friend of mine but not one who makes me stutter.

"He's brave! He's brave! 'Cause he looked at an eighty-year-old lady," said Paul Miller.

There's always one of those loudmouths in a group, and Miller was our loudmouth, always trying to put someone down.

The quiet Maria spoke up, saying, "If it's no big deal, Paul, then why don't you go to Miss Sherwin's house and stare into her eyes. I dare you."

"You gotta be joking."

"I seriously dare you," Mark jumped in.

"Well, ah, OK I'll do it. I mean, it's no biggy, she's, like, older than dust." He was dared. What else could he say but, "I'll do it."

We were giving Miller the guidelines when Geoff Myer came flying down the boardwalk on his green mountain bike.

"Hey, you guys!" he screamed as he skidded to a stop. "You guys! You guys! You guys, guess what?"

"What?"

"There's an ambulance and a cruiser in front of old lady Sherwin's house!"

"What happened?" everyone at the beach echoed.

"I don't know but I think she's dead. I gotta get back there." Geoff got back on his bike and pedaled as fast as his freckled legs could go, smiling to himself with the knowledge that he broke the story to the beach crowd. A group of six of us followed Geoff as if he were the Pied Piper until we came upon the flashing red-and-white lights. Sergeant Gonestone had out a pen and pad and was asking my mom questions. My mom's face was flushed; I could tell she had been crying.

"Mom, are you OK?"

"Oh, Orville!" She left Sergeant Gonestone's side and rushed over to me and gave me a hug.

"Oh, it's terrible, Orville. Poor Miss Sherwin is dead."

Sergeant Gonestone, who had the compassion of a Nazi war criminal, snapped, "Orville, can't you see I'm trying to conduct an investigation here?"

"Oh, I'm so sorry, Sergeant. I thought they recovered the missing Santa."

I was referring to an incident the previous Christmas where Gonestone's son was caught after he stole the town's plastic Santa Claus from the village display.

"You're one wise little piece of ..."

"Any more questions, Sergeant Gonestone?" my mother interrupted. The sergeant grunted at me and turned his attention back to my mom.

"Yes, Mrs. Jacques, you say the door was open?"

"No. It wasn't open. It was unlocked because when I put the key in to open the door I locked it instead, and that's really strange because Miss Sherwin always kept her door locked."

"Yes, I see." Sergeant Gonestone jotted the information on a pad. He was trying too hard to look as if he knew what he was doing. I mean, this was the same man who knocked on every door in Belltown on Christmas Eve in search of a plastic Santa, only to come home greeted by a group of carolers making a citizens' arrest of his own son. They caught Gonestone's son hiding jolly old St. Nick in the shed.

Sergeant Gonestone clearly did not know what he was doing, but he had seen enough prime-time cop shows to end his questioning this way: "If you remember anything, please let me know. In fact, I might have you come down to the station for a few more questions."

"Instead of me going down to the station for questions, why don't you come over tonight for dinner?" my mother offered.

"Oh, really, I couldn't," the sergeant replied, a typical answer from a divorced man who was dying for a home-cooked meal.

"We're having roast beef and apple brown betty for dessert."

"Well, I don't think I'm busy tonight. I'll come over."

I wanted to say, "What about that Hungry Man Dinner in the fridge?" But I bit my lip. I knew Sergeant Gonestone would open his mouth about the case after some tender roast beef in gravy. But then again, I had to admit, maybe there was no case at all.

Sergeant Gonestone devoured the roast beef like a shark, slurping up every ounce of blood. His hands grabbed at rolls, potatoes, gravy, everything except the napkins. I knew a good meal would make him treat even me half decently, so I asked him about the case. He replied, "It was a case of an old woman who had fallen."

As cruel as it is, I wanted to say, "and she couldn't get up." But I kept my mouth shut and let him give every detail.

"You see, old lady Sherwin . . ." my mom flashed him a look and he stopped in mid-sentence. "I mean, Miss Sherwin was getting out of her bathtub and lost her balance. As she was falling down, she tried grabbing a shelf hanging by the tub. The problem was, though, she knocked the shelf off the wall, sending the radio that was on the shelf into the tub. She electrocuted herself."

The chewing at the table stopped, except for Gonestone's.

My father, mother, brother, and sister sat there motionless. All I kept thinking was how could I have thought of a joke about an old woman's death—and such a horrible death, at that.

Gonestone continued his mouth-filled explanation. "She also banged her head on the tub when she fell, leaving a deep wound," he said.

Suddenly, the roast beef wasn't so appetizing.

"She wouldn't have felt that though, because the electric shock probably killed her before that."

"OK, OK, how about some apple brown betty and some ice cream?" My mom was desperately trying to change the subject, but something was tearing at me—something so obvious.

"Sergeant, I have a question about the case."

"Case? I wouldn't call it a case. It's pretty clear-cut, but go ahead and ask me, Orville."

"Miss Sherwin was deaf, right?"

Gonestone let out a sardonic laugh, but I wasn't going to let it faze me.

"Very good observation, Orville."

"OK, then why would she own a radio, never mind have one plugged in on the shelf near her bathtub?"

Gonestone was in mid-swallow when he began to choke. He pointed to the glass in front of him and my dad began to fill it with spring water. Dad turned his attention back to me, saying, "Good point, Orville. That is pretty strange. There was no reason for her to have a radio. It's not as if she had grandkids or friends come over."

It was obvious to everyone at the table except for one of Belltown's finest. He knew he had overlooked the obvious; perhaps this was not the clear-cut case he had described five minutes before. He savored his water for a few seconds before answering, "Well, we are looking into why Miss Sherwin owned a radio."

"What make was the radio?" my dad jumped in on the questioning.

"Huh?"

"Was it old or new?" My eight-year-old brother, Billy, translated for Gonestone.

"Yeah, Sergeant, was it an antique that Miss Sherwin had had for years, or was it a modern radio?" my sister Jackie quizzed.

"Well, ah ... Gonestone had no clue, so he went with the standard, I-have-no-clue response. "That information is classified."

He then looked down at his watch. "Wow! Look at the time. I really gotta get going."

"Can't you stay for dessert?" my mom asked.

"I'd really love to, but that escapee is still on the loose, and we have to have as many people as we can out there looking for him. I think we're closing in on him."

"Closing in?" said my dad.

"Yes. Mrs. Lyons up the street said that she saw a man that fits Walter's description run through her yard last night."

"Sergeant."

"What now, Orville?"

"You mean Mrs. Lyons who lives two doors down the street from Miss Sherwin?"

"You know that's who I mean."

"You're right. What I should say is, do the words 'foul play' mean anything to you?"

"We haven't ruled out anything."

"Yeah, but just a minute ago you said it was a clear-cut case."

My mother came to Gonestone's rescue, saying, "Orville, Jackie did the dishes last night. Now it's your turn."

At that moment, I forgot about Miss Sherwin, Walter, and Sergeant Gonestone. I had to do the dishes and that meant I'd be late for the yacht club teen dance. Gonestone thanked my parents and went on his bewildered way. Once the door was shut, Dad said, "Can you believe that guy?"

"Well, even I have to admit he's no Sherlock Holmes. But I feel very sorry for him what with his divorce and all. That's why I invited Sergeant Gonestone over for dinner," said Mom.

"Mom, the guy's an idiot."

That was the wrong thing to say.

"Orville, you have to understand where Sergeant Gonestone is coming from. His father drank and abused him, and his mother abandoned him at an early age, so you shouldn't judge him as a bad person. I also didn't like the way you talked down to him implying he is stupid."

"Well . . ." Dad laughed.

"You're a big help."

"I'm just kidding," my dad said. Then he continued, "Anyway, you have to admit that Orville may have stumbled onto something here. Maybe it's a real-live murder mystery." He winked at me as he finished speaking.

As I watched my dad walk away, I realized I got my sense of adventure from my dad. He was not thinking of the danger that was involved in having a killer on the loose. He was thinking of the excitement—just like a teenager, just like me. My mind wanted to race with thoughts of who Walter was and whether he killed Miss Sherwin, but I put those thoughts on hold. As I poured the dishwashing liquid on the last pan, I had thoughts of Maria and that famous smile of hers. Maybe tonight I could stutter a few words about the case to her. After all, that morning she seemed interested about my sighting Miss Sherwin. Now I could use this information to my advantage.

Chapter Two

I FINISHED THE dishes using the old "pans have to soak" trick. Dressing was easy. I put on the same jean shorts and the same green Gap T-shirt I had worn the night before. I could get away with wearing the same outfit because I didn't see Maria the night before, and she was all that mattered to me. I didn't care if my friends thought I was a grub, because for the most part, I am. I splashed on some of my dad's cologne, and then went outside, jumped on my mountain bike and headed for the Belltown Yacht Club. The Yacht Club was a ten-minute bike ride. I got there in five minutes. Mark was outside the club, pacing back and forth.

"Where have you been, man?"

"We had Gonestone over for dinner. Guess who got stuck with the dishes?"

"What a bummer! Hey, did you find out anything new about the case?"

"Yeah, but I'll tell you later. I wanna get in there."

"Yeah, you better get in there 'cause a lot of girls

passed me while I was waiting for you."

I locked my bike and we headed inside when Joe shouted at us, "Hey, Jedis! Jedis!"

"What, Joe?" we chanted.

"Oh, ah, do you two Jedis have fifty cents for a fellow Jedi to borrow?"

"What for, Joe? You're way too young to get into the teen dance," Mark laughed.

"I don't want to go to that stupid dance. I wanna get a sundae. I'm almost there. I just need fifty more cents. Please!"

"God, what are you, Joe? An ice-creamaholic?" I said, while checking my pockets for change. I turned out my pockets and realized the firecrackers and matches from the night before were still there.

"Sorry, Joe. This is all I have. Just this and three bucks I brought to get in."

Mark went through his pockets. "Joe, all I have is thirty-five cents."

"I'll take it. Thanks, Jedi." Joe lunged at the quarter and dime and then turned his attention away from us and onto Mickey Wilson.

"Hey, Mickey, do you have a dollar or two I could borrow?"

"Let me check," said Mickey as he rummaged through his pockets.

Mark interrupted, "Hey, don't you only need another fifteen cents?"

"Well, I did, but at the rate I'm going I might get enough for two Reese's Pieces sundaes." He winked. Mark

and I just shook our heads and walked past the panhan-
dling Joe.

The dance was on the third floor of the Yacht Club,
with a dance floor on the inside and a deck outside overlooking the Atlantic Ocean. It was an unwritten law among
dance-goers: The only time you go out on the deck is if
you're going to kiss. Needless to say, I couldn't tell if there
was a good view of the ocean from the deck or not. Mark
told me it was a beautiful view. He seemed to make the
journey to the deck almost every dance. Every dance, I
was too busy doing the same pathetic thing—watching
Maria. This night was no exception. I spotted her across
the dance floor. Mark stood next to me, scanning the floor
like a fighter pilot looking for his target. Top-40 sugar-
coated music was pumping away, while the strobe lights
bounced off the walls. Maria was dancing with a group of
girls. I never understood why girls dance with girls. Almost all the guys were hanging on the walls. Many were
nodding and pointing. They pretended they were a group
of hunters, getting ready to stalk. The reality was that the
girls controlled the hunt and most of us resembled the
petrified deer, especially me! My eyes were fixed on Maria.
She must have felt someone watching her because she
looked in my direction. I looked away in embarrassment.
After a few seconds, I looked back and she was smiling. I
had that "good sick" feeling again. I kept saying to myself,
Stay in control, Orville. You're the man. You're the man. I
flashed back a half smile at her. Her smile got even wider.
She was giving me "the look." I didn't get "the look" much,
but I knew it when I got it, and Maria was definitely giving

me "the look." I knew the move I had to make was to wait for the next slow song and ask her to dance. Mark then nudged me, "Orville, did you see that?"

"What?" I said, not taking my eyes off Maria.

"What you're looking at right now, Maria Simpkins. She's been giving me 'the look' for five minutes, now."

"What do you mean?" I said, in shock.

"A couple of minutes ago I spotted her and waved and blew her a kiss. She's been staring at me ever since."

I was going to protest when the D.J. suddenly cut off the fast song and said in a deep voice, "Let's slow it down a bit, if you know what I mean."

Mark slipped a breath mint into his mouth, patted me on the back, and said, "Wish me luck, bro," as he walked toward Maria. I wanted to stop him and say, "You're no bro of mine, you backstabber," but I couldn't call my best friend a backstabber. I never told him how I felt about Maria. I never told anyone. Mark was using his normal approach. He said something funny. She laughed. He took her hand and led her onto the dance floor. He had done this a dozen times, and I always watched, cheering him on, wishing I had his guts. This time was different. This was Maria! I felt as if I were witnessing a car accident and there was nothing I could do but watch in horror. The cheesy "I will love you forever" type of slow song didn't seem to end. Mark was looking into Maria's brown eyes, and it looked like it wouldn't be long until they kissed. I have to do something before this goes any further, I said to myself.

"Well, well, if it isn't Mr. Jacques." The voice of the chaperone shook me out of my trance. The chaperone was the *beloved* math teacher and wannabe-yachtsman, Mr. Reasons. He was wearing a captain's hat, the kind you buy in a tourist shop, a blue button-down shirt with a red bow tie, and pants I won't even try to describe, except to say they had boats on them.

"Hello, Mr. Reasons," I said in a monotone voice.

"Hello, Mr. Jacques. I hope you don't stay out too late tonight."

"Why's that, Mr. Reasons?"

"Because you have to deliver the papers tomorrow."

"Oh, yeah," I said, half-listening.

Mr. Reasons kept talking to me about something to do with numbers. I was too busy watching the two love-birds. It was driving me crazy. Would they walk towards the deck after the song or would she thank him for the dance and walk away? Finally, the song ended. Mark and Maria headed towards the door to the deck. I was feeling weak and frantic at the same time. I had to do something. I couldn't go outside and third-wheel it. It would be too obvious.

Just then, Mr. Reasons gave me a better gift than an A—or for that matter, a passing grade—on a math test.

"Mr. Jacques, you don't look too well."

"Yeah, yeah."

"Maybe you should go on the deck and get some fresh air."

I laughed. I had found my answer to the equation.

Mark plus Maria plus Mr. Reasons equals three. Three equals no hookup.

"Mr. Reasons, you know I can't go out on the deck."

"Why's that, Mr. Jacques?" he asked.

"You know what they do out there."

"No. Who? What?"

"Well, I'm not supposed to tell you."

"Speak up, Mr. Jacques."

"Well, you didn't hear it from me."

"I didn't hear it from you, Mr. Jacques," he assured me.

"The boys take the girls on the deck to, y'know, kiss. In fact, there go two now," I said as I pointed at Mark and Maria.

I know, I know. I sold out. I'm a sellout. I had to, though. I had no choice; my best friend was going to kiss the girl of my dreams. I knew I could count on Mr. Reasons to come through for me. Reasons, who had lived with his mother all of his life, was not going to allow any of that behavior. He raced through the crowd on the dance floor and grabbed the mike from the D.J.

"Miss Simpkins and her companion, do not go through the door, and that goes for anyone else who might be contemplating the same thing."

"Why?" someone yelled.

"Why? Because . . . because the deck needs to be repaired. Thank you." He wiped his brow.

All attention was on Mark and Maria. Maria was visibly embarrassed as she quickly walked away from Mark and joined her friends. Mark approached me, dejected, "Can you believe that, Orville? We were five feet away from the deck," he said.

"Yeah, tough break, bro."

Maria avoided Mark for the rest of the night. Part of me was psyched. I broke it up. But another part of me knew that if they liked each other, it was going to happen sooner or later. I suppose if she had to pick someone other than me, I guess I'd want her to pick my best friend. That's crazy! Who am I trying to kid? If she didn't want me, I wanted her to wear a habit and clutch a bible to her heart!

Mark and I both decided to leave the dance, each of us for different reasons. I was depressed about Maria. Mark wanted to leave because he knew every girl had seen him heading to the deck with Maria and that meant he really couldn't approach any other girl. We got on our bikes and headed for home. Mark kept talking about Maria, a girl who he had never thought twice about a few hours before. I just kept yessing and yupping, trying to hold in my anger. I think he could sense I was getting annoyed because he finally changed the subject.

"So, Orville, what happened with Gonestone? Did you get any information about the case?"

Normally, Mark would have been the first person I'd tell, but on this night, I couldn't even look at him without getting sick with anger.

"No, I didn't find out anything. It's a pretty clear-cut case. Old lady Sherwin slipped and fell and hit her head on the tub and died. Nothing that special."

"Oh, I thought you said you found something out."

"No, I meant I found out firsthand how Gonestone conducts an investigation."

At that moment, we came to the fork in the road. Mark had to turn left. I had to go right.

"Well, later Orville."

"Yeah, later."

"Are you mad at me or something?" Mark detected.

"No. Not at all, Mark," I lied.

I picked up speed as I passed old lady Sherwin's house, glanced at it quickly. It was in complete darkness. The house was scary enough during the day, never mind at night. And now with the knowledge that old lady Sherwin may have been murdered there, the house took on a whole new meaning of scary. I came to the realization that it was 11:30 at night and I was by myself. The cold sweat from the dance began its warm up again. From my own detective work I had found out that there could be a killer on the loose, and even if Walter wasn't a killer, he had escaped from a mental home and could jump out at any time. I pulled into my driveway, trying not to think about Walter, old lady Sherwin, Maria, and Mark. Think about the Red Sox, I said to myself while locking my bike to the sun deck. Then I realized that was just as scary and depressing—they were six games back and it wasn't even all-star break. As I finished locking my bike, I heard a gagging sound coming from the sidewalk. I waited a couple of seconds, just listening to the most horrible sound. It was the sound of death, I thought. I didn't know if I should approach the figure, in fear that it could be Walter, but then again it could be another one of his victims. As I walked closer to the figure, the gagging stopped, and then I heard it say "Oh, no!" At this point, I could see the figure much clearer. It wasn't Walter and it wasn't another victim. The figure was much smaller up close. The figure was none other than Joe Clancy.

"Joe, are you OK?"

"Ah yeah . . . I'm OK . . . I'm ah, . . . was . . ." Joe didn't know how to say it. He didn't have to say it. We both looked down at his feet and on the sidewalk. Joe had painted his white sneakers and the sidewalk orange.

"Joe, you puked."

"Thanks for pointing that out, Jedi. I don't think I would have figured that out," he said sarcastically.

Joe was never sarcastic so I knew he said this out of embarrassment.

"Joe, what I mean is . . . are you all right? Do you need any help?"

"No, thanks. I'll be OK, but could . . ." he paused.

"Could you do me a favor and not tell anyone you saw me, y' know?"

"Yeah, no problem. Everyone pukes now and then."

"Oh, I know that, Jedi. It's just that I had a bet with Geoff Myer that I could eat three Reese's Pieces sundaes. I downed them one after another. So, if he finds out I barfed them up fifteen minutes later, I'll lose the bet."

"Don't worry, Joe, your secret's safe with me. What do you win?"

"A Reese's Pieces sundae."

"Oh," I nodded.

That was Joe. Tomorrow he would collect on his bet and eat that Reese's Pieces sundae as if nothing ever happened. I was trying to do some ice-cream intervention by telling him maybe he should cut down on eating so much when he began pointing at old lady Sherwin's house. "Did you see that?"

"What?"

"That!" he pointed again.

That time I saw it! It was a light shining through old lady Sherwin's downstairs. It had to be a flashlight. We ran over to the fence, jumped it, and looked into the window. Two guys were whispering to each other, flashing the light on objects and picking and choosing what they wanted. They were so casual about their stealing, discussing the quality of the grandfather clock and the value of the wine glasses.

I turned to Joe, "We gotta do something, Joe!"

"What? Orville, I'm scared. They could have knives or guns."

"I know, I know, . . ." I was trying to think of a plan.

"We should go wake your parents."

"No, my parents aren't home. They went to the town band concert."

"Wait!" I snapped my fingers. I had a plan.

"Joe, let's go to my house."

We jumped the fence and burned to my house.

"OK, Joe, you call the cops and tell them what's going on."

"Yeah, but they might take forever. What are you gonna do, anyway?"

I took the keys to the old blue car off the key hanger.

"What are you doing? You don't have your license."

"Minor detail, Joe. Anyway, I've been practicing with my dad."

"Well, what are you going to do with the car?"

"Stall them. So hurry up and call the cops."

I really didn't know what I was going to do, and why I was jumping into my dad's old clunker was beyond me. I just did it. Some force that I couldn't describe made me do it. I started up the car and slowly backed out onto the street. I put my foot down on the gas, maybe a little too much, because I went beyond old lady Sherwin's driveway and onto the grass. "Now what?" I thought. I flashed on the high beams so the robbers would be blinded. Then I decided to put my acting talent to work.

"Come on outside, boys, we know you're in there." I got out of the car, threw my voice in the theater sense and made it hoarse-sounding; I wasn't going to win an Academy Award, but it worked. The robbers waited a few seconds and then busted out of the back door. They were going to make a run for it. "The firecrackers," I blurted to myself. I pulled them out of my pocket, lit the whole pack, and tossed them against the fence on the lawn. Both men revised their strategy and dove to the ground to eat dirt.

"All right! All right! We're not going anywhere!"

"Yeah, don't shoot! We're not going anywhere, you crazy. . ."

"I thought you boys would see it our way," I growled, though I wanted to laugh.

Two cruisers flew past me and boxed in the two would-be robbers. The men in blue leaped out of their cars and cuffed them immediately.

Gonestone sauntered over to the men and began giving them the old Gonestone shakedown. The robbers were pointing at me. I turned off the high beams, and the robbers could see now that I was not a Belltown policeman but a teenager who enjoyed playing with firecrackers. They were not amused. I have to admit I was pretty proud of myself. I was smiling uncontrollably, but I was also shaking with nervous excitement. The cops were reading the criminals their rights in the backyard, so I was the only person to see the front door open. A gray-haired man slithered out the door and started to creep across the street. He suddenly stopped and looked back and caught me watching.

I knew immediately who the man was. It was Walter. I wanted to yell or scream to Gonestone, but nothing came out. Walter put his index finger to his mouth as if to say, "Sh." He didn't have to worry about me trying to play hero again. My nervous excitement had turned into flat-out fear as I watched him jump into the bushes and disappear into the night.

Just then I realized Joe was standing at my side.

"Jedi, we did it. We caught them."

"Yeah, we did. Didn't we, Joe?" I gave one last look at the bushes.

"Orville, those two apparently thought you were a policeman," said Gonestone.

I figured even Gonestone had to give me some credit for helping them catch the bad guys. I figured wrong.

"Orville, did you shoot at those guys?" Gonestone continued.

I started to laugh. "No, Sergeant, I pretended I did. I lit some firecrackers and told them I was a cop—I mean, policeman."

"Wow! That's awesome!" said Joe.

"Joe, could you let Orville and me talk alone?"

"Sure, Sergeant."

"Oh, Joe, good job calling us. That was the right thing for you to do."

Joe looked at me and then at Gonestone, and said, "Yeah, no problem, sergeant."

"OK, Jacques, so you impersonated an officer and set off some firecrackers, pretending they were bullets. Do you know what kind of danger you put yourself in? What if we pulled in when those firecrackers were going off? We probably would have drawn our guns. And what if the robbers had guns and decided to shoot back at your fire-crackers? And also, Jacques, it's against the law to imper-sonate an officer."

"Aw, sergeant, I was just trying to help."

"You would have helped if you did the responsible thing as Joe Clancy did. He called us and we did our job. Another thing, do you have your license?"

"Well, no."

"So now you're operating a vehicle without a license. I could charge you for that. But I won't, because your mother doesn't deserve that kind of trouble."

"Sergeant, I might not have thought about the conse-quences if my plan didn't work, but aren't you forgetting that I did help you catch those guys?"

"Orville, you didn't help at all. Y' know why? They said when they were running out of the house they saw another man in the house. Their description matched Walter's. If you didn't play cops and robbers, we would have caught him, too. So don't think you're the town hero, kid. You're just a royal pain in the . . ."

My parents' car pulled up, interrupting Gonestone's endless praise.

I went to bed that night with the knowledge that my best friend liked the girl of my dreams, that I had caught two robbers and that I wasn't given any credit for that. I also doubted that Miss Sherwin's death was accidental. And the prime suspect was an escapee from a mental hospital, and he knew I had seen him. Let's just say that I didn't get much sleep.

Chapter Three

It was 5:30 in the morning, and it was already seventy-three degrees. Lying under the covers was no place to escape the heat, so I decided I might as well face it. Besides, it was the last day I had to get up so early. I went downstairs and brought the papers in. The headline said: "Long-time Belltown Resident Found Dead." The article said how my mom suspected that there was something wrong and contacted the police. It continued, "The police found the body and believed Miss Sherwin died as a result of an accidental fall." *What other kind of fall is there?* Of course, I knew what the reporter meant; Miss Sherwin fell, she wasn't pushed. There was no mention of the radio, and I wondered if today the cops would change their tune about the "accidental fall." I also wondered if my involvement in catching two robbers would be mentioned in the next day's *Belltown News*. I don't know why I wondered that. I knew the answer: No. They would write about Joe Clancy calling the police, and then every other word would be Gonestone.

I was somewhat nostalgic on my last day as a paper-boy. I had had the route for four years; giving it up was like saying goodbye to part of my life. Oh, well. I was kind of surprised how quiet it was in my neighborhood. It was only quarter of six, but I figured with the heat, people would be up. If there was any morning to eat a Creamsicle, this was one, and Joe wasn't even up! He was probably still sleeping off the sundaes. I got on my bike and decided I owed Mr. Reasons, whether he knew it or not, so I delivered the first paper to his house. I thought I would hit my customers by the beach so I could get some of that Belltown ocean breeze. I quickly realized that the cool Belltown breeze was going to take the day off. This was going to be a day that, if you weren't going to the beach, you'd better take refuge at the dentist's office, where there was some air-conditioning. Who would want to be there? I rode along, debating whether I should tell Mark and my parents that I had seen Walter the night before. My parents would appreciate the adventure, but in the end they were my parents and would be concerned about my safety. They might get so concerned that they'd give me a curfew! I didn't want to tell Mark because I was mad at—and jealous of—him. Then I thought of all the times we sat around his patio, listening to the radio, drinking soda and eating Cape Cod chips, telling one another ghost stories and mysteries. We always ended the night saying, "Why can't there be any mysteries in Belltown?" Now I might have stumbled onto a real-life murder mystery, and I didn't want to tell my best friend because of a girl. Grow up, Orville! I said to myself as I approached the halfway point of my route.

Now that I had made my decision, I couldn't wait to tell Mark. As I passed the boardwalk, a body stepped off the boardwalk into my path. I pushed down on my brakes hard and almost wiped out. Walter stood about two feet in front of me, breathing hard. He must have never used a toothbrush; his teeth were a sick yellow. As he panted in my face, his breath reeked.

Walter slowly pulled his hands out of the pockets of his Bermuda shorts and wrapped them around my handle-bars. His face wore a blank, distant look. His green eyes just stared at me for what seemed like hours. I know that's such a cliche but believe me—it felt that way! I was eye-to-eye with an escaped mental patient—a crazy man who had killed an old lady and knew I thought he had done it. So, if he knocked off an old lady, what was going to stop him from doing the same to a defenseless teenager? His knuckles were white as he kept a tight grip on my handle-bars. I made a vain attempt to pull my bike loose. But he didn't do anything. He just stared. I was petrified for the first minute; then I began to get annoyed. If he was going to do something, I wanted him to do it quick. The staring thing got a little old, so I finally blurted out, "What do you want from me?" But it came out more this way, "Whadya . . . ahhh . . . fro' me?" It looked as though he was going to answer when we saw flashing lights coming from about two hundred yards up the street. I could see this caught Walter totally off guard. He had to make his point and make it quick.

"Boy, you don't talk. You see me?" He let go of my bike and pointed to his chest.

I managed a weak,"Yeah."

"No! You didn't see me."

I nodded and he gave me a glare before he jogged up the boardwalk and jumped off the beach wall and vanished behind the dunes.The flashing lights came closer. I couldn't believe that for the second day in a row I was relieved to see Gonestone and his boys. Then I realized that the lights weren't blue and white but yellow. It was the Belltown Beach Committee trash truck making its daily rounds."I should've known better," I said out loud.

"Hey, Orville!" the group of three yelled.

"Hey, what's up, boys?" I was trying to hide my fear, but I really felt as if I was going to faint.

"We heard about you, Orville," said Dan Francais.

We called him Franco.

"What's that, Franco?" I managed.

"How you caught the guys trying to break into old lady Sherwin's last night."

"Me and the boys were just at Bill's Donuts, so we're sitting there—" Franco couldn't finish the story because Scotty Donovan, who loved telling stories, interrupted and took over, saying "Yeah, so we're sitting there, Orville. Man, you're gonna love this, Orville. We're sitting there and Gonestone is going on and on about how he caught the robbers using his new K-9."

"What? That dog wasn't even around!" I said, disgusted.

"Yeah, I know, man. Now listen. So he's going on how he was driving by old lady Sherwin's and the dog reacted. Like everybody is getting into his story and Gonestone is loving it. You know Gonestone, he's eating it up. The only thing he didn't know was that your dad was at the counter, picking up some donuts. So your dad says, 'Did you mention what my son did, Sergeant?' You should've seen Gonestone's face. He was like 'Huh?' It was classic! So everybody asked 'What'd he do? What'd he do?' So your dad told the story. And of course, we all believed your dad cause he's about the most honest guy in town."

For that brief moment I had to smile. My old man was protecting my back. He wasn't going to let Gonestone get away with his lies. And that was my problem— Gonestone's lies. I would tell him about Walter if I knew I could trust him and that he could keep it low-key, but those were two things the man wasn't capable of doing.

For the next ten minutes I gave my version of the story to Scotty, Franco, and the summer kid who was with them. I knew it was the first of many times I'd tell the story that day.

Scotty listened intently. He would probably tell the story even more than me. With Scotty Donovan as an endorser, I was going to become something of a small-town celebrity. I could live with that. What I couldn't live with was the idea that a crazed killer was threatening me. The reality of that set in when the beach committee trash truck drove away, leaving me alone again. Or was I? I looked towards the dunes, but I didn't see him. I took a deep breath and tried to regain my composure. I had to straighten out my newspapers before I could ride out of there. That's when I saw it. There was something lying on the ground in front of me. I picked it up and studied it. It was a stub of folded paper. I unfolded it to discover it was an order receipt. It read: #S41883/ Mario's Camera Store/ Martha's Vineyard, MA. Anybody could have dropped the receipt, but I knew it wasn't anybody. It came to me at that moment—a snippet of a memory, but it was a memory. When Walter pulled his hands out of his shorts pockets, the stub fell to the ground. I saw it happen, but I didn't take much notice of it at the time. I was more concerned about other things, like whether he was going to kill me. Now I knew this stub could be just as important. It was my first clue.

By the time I got to the beach, the word was out how I caught the two robbers. I knew this had to get me some points with Maria. I was telling my story to the usual group of listeners, but I didn't get into it as I had done when I told them I had seen Miss Sherwin. The only person I wanted to be interested wasn't. Maria was sitting on the beach wall, laughing at every word Mark uttered. I had the attention of the whole beach, I was a hero among my peers—and Maria was more interested in Mark's knock-knock jokes. I tried to rationalize the fact that the girl wasn't interested in me. She had no personality. Who needed her? Mark could have her, for all I cared. Of course, I didn't really believe any of these things. But rejection is much easier to swallow when you decide you don't like the person who rejects you. That is why it was easy walking up to Mark and Maria without being nervous. I had to talk to Mark, and I wasn't going to let some girl make me wait. As I approached, their laughter died down.

"Hi, Orville." Maria gave me her usual beautiful smile,

but I wasn't going to let that intimidate me. I gave her the old, "Yeah, hi" response, as if I didn't care. I continued "Hey, Mark, I gotta talk to you."

"About what, Orville?" Mark gave me the "leave us alone" look.

I understood the look, and as much as it angered me I wasn't going to cause a scene.

"It's private," I said as I looked at Maria.

"I can leave," Maria said.

"No. No. You two do what you were doing. I'm going home right now. But Mark, can you come over to tonight?" I asked, trying to ignore Maria.

"Yeah, I can come by, but it will be around eleven. Maria and I are going to Dailey's Roast Beef and then to the movies." He gave me a smile.

Do you want to stick the knife in a little deeper? was what I wanted to say; instead I said, "Yeah, eleven would be OK."

I turned to walk away when, as always, Maria's voice froze me in mid-step.

"Orville." I turned to face her.

"I heard about you catching the robbers. Great job! You're a regular hero." Her smile was irresistible. As terrible as I felt, I wanted to smile, but I bit the side of my mouth, and said rudely, "Yeah, whatever," and walked away.

On summer nights in Belltown, the harbor is the place to be. Other than an occasional fight, nothing ever exciting happened out there. That didn't matter, though, because everyone hung out there. I hung out there for a little while and told my story to a few more listeners. To tell the truth, I was getting sick of the story, and I was getting sick of hearing my own voice. I went home and grabbed a soda out of the fridge and put on my Walkman and headed for the sun deck. Whenever I want to relax and leave my troubles behind, the Walkman and a good mixed tape always do the trick. For a little while I was able to forget Walter and my lack of any social life. Then Mark pulled into my yard on his bike and brought it all back. He tried telling me about his date, but I told him there was a more pressing matter to discuss.

"What I'm going to tell you I haven't told anyone, and I'm not supposed to tell anyone," I gave him a serious look.

"Yeah, we're best friends, that's the way it goes," Mark said.

"I know that, but if you know what I know, it might put you in a lot of danger. But you can't tell anyone even if you don't want to help me."

"Come on, Orville. You know you can trust me," Mark said. "I came face to face with Walter, and he threatened me."

I think Mark was expecting me to say something like, "I have a crush on the head lifeguard." He couldn't believe it. I told him everything, including how I thought Walter had killed Miss Sherwin.

"What I don't understand is, if Walter killed Miss Sherwin, why is he sticking around town?" I asked Mark.

"Yeah, even if he didn't kill her, he's still a fugitive. Fugitives run; they don't stay in one place," Mark pointed out.

"Exactly, that's why I think there's more to this. And as much as common sense tells me to stay out of it, I can't. So are you gonna help me, Mark? In or out?" I put my hand out.

"What do you think? Of course I'm in." He shook my hand.

"Now, Mark, you better go home and get some sleep. You start delivering papers tomorrow," I laughed.

"Wow, you're cold, man. Hey, do you start at the Island Princess tomorrow?"

"No, I have three more days of freedom. But I'll be up early. I have to make a couple of phone calls," I mused.

"Who?" Mark asked.

"The Bayside Mental Hospital, to ask them about their volunteer program, and Mario's Camera Store, to ask them when we can pick up our photos."

I put up my hand to high-five Mark and we both said, "Awesome!" It was a lot easier going to sleep that night, knowing I was not alone in this thing, whatever this thing was.

The clock in my body rang at 5:45 AM. I was about to get up when it struck me that I didn't have to deliver the papers ever again. It had to be one of the best feelings in the world. I felt giddy with the knowledge I could sleep another three or four hours, and that Mark, the poor fool, was just starting his route. After a few more chuckles, I met the sandman again. It finally rolled out of bed at 9:00 AM. I decided I'd give up doing the three-eggs-in-a-glass thing. I just wasn't working. My arms were skinny and they were going to stay skinny unless I started lifting. That meant going to the gym and facing all the muscleheads who would comment on how I couldn't lift my own weight. Maybe in the fall, I thought. My parents were already up, making breakfast. My mom was making her classic fried potatoes, and my father was making the one thing he knew how to make—pancakes. Yup, every morning for my dad was a pancake morning.

"Hey, it's the town hero!" my dad smiled as he flipped away. "Good morning," I said, still groggy.

"You're in the paper, honey. It mentions how you and Joe called the police," my mom informed me.

"Nothing about the other stuff?" I asked, scanning the paper.

"No, but don't let that bother you. The whole town knows what really happened. Do you want me to put a pancake on for you?" asked my dad, trying to be sympathetic. The only problem was that, over the years, I had had about two thousand pancakes of his, and I couldn't even dream of trying to force another one down.

"No, thanks! I'll have some fried potatoes, though."

"Well, excuse me," Dad said jokingly.

My mother came over to the table and gave me a huge helping of fried potatoes and bacon. She continued the conversation I had interrupted.

"Oh, so I was getting my hair done yesterday, and I

began talking to Cindy Gaudreault, who works at the bank, and we were mentioning what happened to Miss Sherwin. Can you believe Tom Anderson came into the bank and asked when they were going to put the house up for sale?"

"What's so bad about that?" I asked.

"Orville, the lady isn't even buried yet. And already he's trying to get his paws on more land," my mother said, while pouring a glass of orange juice.

"Yeah, that is kind of harsh," I agreed.

"Well, what do you expect? He's a businessman. He has no heart." My dad always said exactly how he felt.

"Why would he want to buy that old house?" I asked. "He owns half of Belltown already."

"Location, Orville. The house may be old and might need some work, but it's right up the street from the beach. Also, since he owns the motel right behind Miss Sherwin's house, he might buy her house so he can resell it to an owner he can trust as far as upkeep and loud parties are concerned. He'll probably look for another Miss Sherwin type of person to buy it."

My father's real estate explanation seemed to make a lot of sense, but it was hard trying to take him seriously about the business world when he had just set off the smoke detector. The room was filled with smoke and the high-pitched sound from the detector, which did not please Ophelia, who barked wildly. Dad was ignoring the whole thing, thinking that maybe we wouldn't say anything. Mom and I couldn't resist.

She gave me a wink and said to Dad, "You know, honey, I realize you're the master of pancakes but something tells me that they might be done."

"Yeah, I think it's your timer," I added.

"Very funny," Dad said, faking anger. But he couldn't help joining in the laughter.

I called the Bayside Mental Hospital and made a three o'clock appointment with Mrs. Harris to talk about the volunteer program. I gave good old Mario's Camera Shop a call and asked when our pictures would be ready. The man at the shop said, "Two days." Either he wasn't the nicest guy or he was expecting me to complain because he went on a tirade about tourists wanting their pictures immediately, that kind of stuff.

Mark and I walked into the mental hospital. We figured there would be a bunch of Charlie Manson types running around yelling "I am Satan" or "Satan Rules." It was actually a very mellow atmosphere. Of course, we were only standing in the lobby. An enthusiastic woman in her early forties greeted us.

"Good afternoon. You must be the boys who inquired about the volunteer program. I'm Mrs. Harris."

"Hi, I'm Orville Jacques."

"Hi, I'm Mark Price."

"You don't know how excited I am to see two young men who are interested in helping. Usually, young people stereotype our guests—we like to call the patients 'guests.' They assume all kinds of behavior, you know, and they don't want to have anything to do with them."

Instantly, I felt guilty because I had no intention of volunteering. The volunteering thing was just a ploy to get us into the hospital to pick this woman's brain about Walter and his past.

She continued, "Why are you interested in helping the mentally challenged? I like to say 'challenged' because 'ill' is so negative—as though there is no hope; but there is hope," her eyes danced.

Mark looked at me. I realized being a private investigator means you sometimes have to leave your ethics at home.

"Well, to tell you the truth, Mrs. Harris, my grandmother was mentally challenged, and after reading about that patient . . . I mean guest . . . what was his name?"

"Walter," she said, looking at me as if I was an angel from heaven.

"Yes, Walter. Reading about him running away just stirred it all up again. I figure if these people had some visitors . . ."

"They wouldn't feel compelled to run away," she finished my sentence.

"Yes. I mean, that man wouldn't have run away unless he was lonely," I nodded.

"Well, Walter is a unique person because he always keeps to himself. He is also a difficult person to help because we don't know his history. We don't know if he has a family. We don't even know his last name. Those are the worst cases because you don't know what the guest is suffering from."

"How could Walter afford it here? This is a private hospital, right?" I asked, digging a little more, maybe too much.

"He was paid up through—wait, enough about Walter. Orville, you told me why you wanted to volunteer. Why do you want to, Mark?" she asked, as she turned to Mark.

Mark hesitated for a minute, and I was afraid he was going to blow it. He didn't have my gift for dramatics, and I figured he was going to say something stupid. Instead, he looked Mrs. Harris in the eye and said, "Why am I here? Orville's my best friend. This is something he has to do, and I'm going to help him do it."

I thought she was going to hug us both. I was trying to rationalize my lying. Hey, Grandma must have been a little mental, after all, she gave me the name Orville.

The intercom interrupted our meeting, and it was a good thing, because I didn't know if I could mention Walter again without being obvious.

"Mrs. Harris, please come to room 342."

"Oh, no. It's Ruth," Mrs. Harris whispered. "Boys, I'm sorry, I really have to see the guest in room 342. She is suffering from severe depression. Why don't you take these pamphlets and get back to me after you've looked them over."

Mrs. Harris gave us both a stack of reading material that could last a couple of weeks.

"Thanks," we nodded.

Mrs. Harris smiled and hurried toward the stairs.

"Not only did we not find out anything about Walter, I feel totally guilty that I lied to Mrs. Harris," I said as I shook my head.

"Oh, so you do have a conscience. I was beginning to wonder after that story about your grandmother," Mark laughed.

"Yeah, me too," agreed a voice from behind us.

Mark and I turned around and saw a man wearing "guest" clothes and a black felt hat, sitting in a chair. His bushy, white eyebrows appeared to keep his hat on his head.

"I'm sorry. I didn't know you were there," I said.

I didn't have to say it but I didn't know what else to say to someone in a mental hospital. The man laughed.

"Why are you apologizing to me? I'm the one who was spying on you two." He pointed at us.

"You got a point there," said Mark, trying to buddy-up to him.

"Why were you spying on us?" I asked.

"Well, normally, I just sit over here and listen to the volunteers for a couple of minutes, and they're usually boring so I'll go back to my reading. You see, I sneak up here to read. I don't read in the common room."

"Why don't you read in the common room?" Mark asked.

The man looked around to see if anyone was watching and then said, "'Cause they're crazy in there."

He let out a laugh, and Mark and I both joined in.

"Anyway, I was going to go back to my reading when I heard you say all that stuff about your grandmother, and then you asked about Walter. Son, I was a private investigator, and I gotta tell you, you're too obvious. I spotted you a mile away." He laughed louder.

"Well, Mrs. Harris didn't catch on," I said, a little offended.

"Dr. Harris is a nice woman, but she's not all there," he said, still giggling.

I wanted to laugh at the irony of this comment, but

instead I asked, "If she's a doctor, why did she introduce herself as Mrs. Harris?"

His laughter started up again; and it was beginning to annoy me, but I could see it had the opposite effect on Mark, who was laughing along. The man mimicked Mrs. Harris's voice, "I call myself Mrs. Harris because the mentally challenged guests won't feel as if they are in a hospital." The impression brought out more laughter from Mark, and I had to admit to myself that the guy was pretty funny.

"OK, let's be serious for a moment. My name is Will, and you're Mark and you're Orville. Where did you get a name like Orville?"

"From my mentally deranged grandmother," I responded.

"You're all right, Orville. Now, why do you want to know about Walter?" The tone in Will's voice became serious.

"Well," I paused and looked at Mark.

"C'mon, Orville, tell him," Mark pleaded.

"Well, I saw Walter face to face, and he threatened me."

Will's eyes popped out. "You mean Walter's still in town?"

"Yeah. This just happened yesterday morning," I answered.

"Tell me everything," he ordered.

I told him it all even though I was a little reluctant telling a complete stranger, a mental one at that.

After I was done, Will nodded, and then said, "First of all, believe his threat. If he told you not to tell anyone, don't. Now I'm going to tell you two something he told me, but you have to keep it to yourselves. Because if he gets caught, he'll come back here, and if he finds out I sang, Bang! That's the show. Got it?"

"Yes."

"We won't talk," said Mark.

"Well, I was the only person Walter talked to because at times I can be pretty rational, other times though . . . well, we won't talk about that. Anyway, he told me he had killed before and he would do it again. He told me he was leaving to do it again. To kill and protect."

"To kill who?"

"And protect what?" Mark and I fired questions at Will.

"I don't know. He wouldn't say. But I'll tell you this much. If he's hanging out around your neighborhood, he's doing it for a reason, and I wouldn't get in his way if I were you."

"You're right, but we have to know," Mark spoke for both of us.

"You two have it in your blood," Will smiled.

"What's that?" I asked.

"The desire to know the truth. The desire to be a PI."

We both shook his hand and thanked him. As we walked toward the door, Will stopped us with a "Hey!" We turned back. His once-laughing eyes now looked lonely. In a weak voice, Will said, "Could you update me if anything happens?"

"Will, you'll be seeing us again real soon. We promise."

Mark and I smiled; Will nodded in appreciation. Before we pulled out of Bayside on our bikes, Mark and I made a pact to visit Will every couple of weeks. To us, when it came to Will, the term "guest" seemed appropriate. When it came to Walter, on the other hand . . . .

Chapter Four

WILL WAS RIGHT. He had spotted my detective style a mile away, and Mark and I really didn't know what we were doing. We were just doing it the way we saw it on TV. On TV, though, the crime was set up, and a couple of clues were given, and after an hour, the crime was solved and the show ended with the main characters laughing. Cut to a commercial. But this was real life. There were no commercials. And after Will told us that Walter had killed and would do it again, none of the main characters were laughing.

We really didn't know how to continue the investigation. We were waiting for the pictures. I started to doubt my memory. What if it wasn't Walter's receipt stub? What if just some tourist dropped it and we were going to pick up pictures of a three-year-old making sand castles? We'd only know once we saw the pictures, and that was another day's wait. It was also my first day at the *Island Princess*. Mark and I both agreed if the pictures didn't give us more clues, we 'd let the whole thing go and hope Walter just moved on. But, if the photos did offer more clues, then it would be too late to turn back. I had that feeling, anyway. I think Mark did, too.

While we were waiting for the day to come, we tried to act like normal teenagers. We went to the beach and watched Joe take up a collection to ride his bike off the beach wall. I put fifty cents into his hat. Joe thought he'd land safely because of the sand. He forgot that it was a four-foot drop. As he landed, his body went over the handlebars, and he ate about a pound of sand. He was coughing and teary-eyed, but he brightened up when he saw his efforts earned him four dollars and twenty-five cents.

After Joe's circus act, Mark and I went back to my house to play our daily Wiffle-ball game. Mark informed me that he was now "seeing" Maria. I always thought that was a stupid phrase to describe a relationship. "I'm seeing Maria." I wanted to say, "Yeah, well I'm seeing her, too, whenever I see her." The seeing thing never made any sense. Either go out, or don't go out—don't see! I guess I get a little excited about this. Anyway, Mark and Maria were now an item, and there was nothing I could do about it but accept the fact that she didn't want me. I wasn't going to do that. So I decided to do the mature thing and ignore it. Yeah, real mature.

It was 7:45 AM when I arrived at the *Island Princess* parking lot. I had on my official *Island Princess* uniform, which consisted of a white, short-sleeved, button-down shirt with the I.P. emblem, and a pair of khaki pants. Yes, pants. No shorts. I didn't like the idea of working in eighty plus heat in pants. But I guess these are the concessions you have to make when you join the working world. The manager who ran the boat and parking lot greeted me. He was a slightly overweight man in his fifties.

"Are you ready for your first day at the Princess?" he asked, smiling.

"Yes, Mr. Thomas." I was a little nervous.

"All right, Orville, a couple of things before you start. First of all, this 'Mr. Thomas' stuff has to go. My nickname is Tommy. So call me Tommy."

"OK, Tommy," I smiled.

"What are all tourists?" He waited for my answer, but I had no idea what he meant. So he continued, "All tourists are right. Even though they're never right. They're almost always wrong, but you have to bite the side of your mouth and let them think they're right, you know why?"

Tommy scratched his head.

"Why, Tommy?"

"Because you're being paid with tourist dollars. Once you realize the meaning of that, you'll be fine. There's one other thing tourists are, but you'll learn that soon enough. When they complain about the price of parking, just say something cute like, 'Gotta save for college,' or 'If I owned this place I'd be sipping soda on a beach somewhere.' Then they'll leave you alone. All right, you know how to sell the parking tickets, so go to it."

He gave me a slap on the back and then headed down to the boat, which was a hundred-and-fifty yards up the street.

I worked with a guy named Boom Boom. He was called that because he boxed in the Navy while serving during World War II. Boom Boom was a great guy and made me feel comfortable right from the beginning. He had lived in Belltown all his life and prided himself on knowing everything about the town's history. During the slow times that day, he told me stories about growing up in Belltown.

As the day went on, I began to realize what Tommy was talking about the other thing tourists were—dumb. I heard some of the most ridiculous questions: "When does the 10:20 boat leave?" "Are there beaches on the island?" "We can't drive to the island?" to quote just a few. At about 1:30 PM. Tommy informed me that the guy who was supposed to relieve me was sick in bed. Could I stay till closing, which was 8:00 PM? I was supposed to go on the three o'clock Island Princess with Mark to get the pictures at Mario's. But this was my first day. How could I say no? There was no way. So I told Tommy, "Sure. No problem. I just have to make a phone call." I called Mario's and told him that # S41883 would pick up the photos tomorrow. He said, "It doesn't matter because they're still not ready."

He then complained about how impatient tourists were. I was beginning to understand Mario's frustration, as a lady yelled at me while I hung up.

"What, ma'am?" I glared at her.

"What time does the three o'clock boat leave?"

"That's what I meant. I hear that one all the time," said Tommy, chuckling.

That night Mark and I met on my sun deck and planned our trip. The next day we would take the three o'clock boat and arrive at the Vineyard at 3:45. We would go to Mario's, get the pictures, and jump on the 4:45 back to Belltown. If the pictures proved to be Walter's or gave us any clues, we would stake out the camera store and watch for Walter. If they didn't give us any information, and I was wrong about Walter dropping the receipt, then we would get an ice cream and wait for the boat and give up our little adventure.

That night I tossed and turned and had mixed feelings about the film. A part of me wanted something on that film that would challenge my senses; I wanted to prove I could face the challenge. But another part of me knew if there was something important on this film, it could mean danger, and I wasn't sure I could face that. I'm not much for going to church, but I am, once in awhile, spiritual. That night before I went to sleep, I tried saying a prayer. And then I realized that if Miss Sherwin didn't die naturally, God might be asking these two teenagers to find the truth. But why me? I said softly. Maybe God tried Gonestone and is now really desperate. Well, if that's the case, why can't I date Maria in return? I stopped. My prayer was going off on a tangent. I did feel better looking at this as a mission from God. I know that sounds a little melodramatic, especially coming from a kid who got thrown out of Sunday School for going to a Red Sox game instead. But, that's how I felt, lying in bed, listening to the midnight crickets singing me to sleep.

Mark went into Mario's Camera Store to make sure no one resembling Walter was in there. I didn't exactly want to bump into him again. Mark opened the door and gave me a little wave to assure me the coast was clear.

Mario's Camera Store was old fashioned or run-down, depending on how you looked at it. The tourists probably thought it was charmingly old-fashioned. I thought it was just a dump. It was dusty, and all the camera equipment for sale was old and outdated. There were no millimeter cameras, video cameras, or even throwaway cameras. The owner must've really hated tourists, because the equipment he had certainly didn't cater to their needs. He was a short, bald man who looked as dated as the equipment on his shelves. His glasses perched on the edge of his nose as he peered at us for a few seconds.

"Well, what do you two want? We don't have any of those silly Polaroid cameras here. You take a picture and you want to see it instantly. That's the problem with society—instant gratification. Everyone's so impatient!"

I stopped his commentary. "You must be Mario."

"No, I'm not Mario," he answered, and looked at me as though I had three heads.

"Then who's Mario?" Mark asked.

"Mario's the one I bought this store from a long time ago. So what do you two want?"

I don't know what this man's hurry was, but his abrupt behavior made me want to get to the point and get out of there.

"Well, my boss gave me this receipt to give to you to pick up his order."

I handed him the receipt and he studied it. His glasses slid to the very tip of his nose; I thought they were going to fall off.

"Oh, yes." He actually almost smiled. "It took me a few days but as I told your boss, I keep all unclaimed orders, and sure enough, I looked through my file cabinets and found that number. Wait one second."

The man went into the back room. Mark and I didn't say anything. We were both holding our breaths, waiting for his return. He came back with a brown envelope. "This envelope used to be white. That's how old these pictures are. They must be forty, fifty, maybe even sixty years old. But I always keep them until they're claimed."

The man handed me the envelope. I checked the outside of the envelope to see how much I owed him for the pictures. I paid him and then I said, "Well, sir, thanks for finding them."

I wanted to open the envelope right on the spot, but we knew we should get out of the store before Walter got there.

We left the store and headed toward Mad Martha's for some root-beer floats to cool off, and then to find a remote place where we could devour the floats and the pictures.

I had the same feeling I get when I open my report card: I want to know what I get, but at the same time I want to be alone, with no distractions. Mark and I went to the halfway point along Oak Bluffs harbor. There was no one around except a vacationing fisherman about fifty yards beyond, trying desperately to bait his hook.

"Are you ready, Orville?"

"Yup."

I rested my float on the jetty and opened the envelope. The first picture was of a young woman smiling and holding onto a little baby. I analyzed it for a few seconds and handed it to Mark. The second one was of a pond in the foreground and a cabin in the background. The third picture was of a man sitting behind an oak desk. On the desk was a name marker, but the name was blurred. I could only make out the first word, Mayor. The man in the photo wore no expression on his face—just a cold stare. The rest of the pictures were of the young woman with the baby in different poses—on her lap, crawling beside her, on her shoulders, and so on. When I looked closely at the young woman's face, I realized she was probably not even eighteen. She only looked older and motherly because she was dressed so formally and she was holding a little baby. In one of the poses, the girl pretended the baby and she were dancing cheek to cheek. Something about her seemed familiar.

"What do you make of this?" Mark said, with disappointment in his voice. I think he was expecting a gun, a dead body, or something else fantastic. I shouldn't put him down because that's the kind of thing I expected, too.

"I guess it would help if we knew who these people were. But something about the girl is familiar to me. I just can't quite figure out what it is."

I squinted as I studied her smiling face, but then I concentrated on her eyes. The eyes weren't smiling. They were concerned, narrow. I had seen that look before.

"That's Miss Sherwin!"

"What? How do you know that?"

"I just do. I know her eyes. They had that look of fear

or concern, or something. I know those eyes, Mark."

"How can you say fear or concern? The girl in the picture is smiling."

"Yeah, yeah, I know. But block her smile and just look at her eyes."

Mark obeyed and put his index finger on her mouth and stared for a few seconds.

"Yeah, but Orville, all old black-and-white pictures look kind of scary if you look just at the eyes."

"Yeah, you're right, but I know that 'scary.' I saw that fear in Miss Sherwin's eyes when she pointed at me to get out of her yard. She was like a black-and-white picture. I'm telling you, it's Miss Sherwin!"

Mark asked the obvious question, which I hadn't even thought of—"Then who's the baby?"

"Oh, my God! I don't know. She was an only child, right?"

"Orville, you know the story about Miss Sherwin having an illegitimate child?"

"That's it!"

"Yeah, maybe it's not just a story."

"You're right. It might not be a story at all. But . . .

"But what?"

"Well, even though I'm positive it's Miss Sherwin in these pictures, we should try to confirm it."

"Yeah, you're right. That should be our next move."

The *Island Princess's* horn blew as it entered the harbor.

"What time is it?" he asked.

"Can you believe it's 4:35?"

"Wow, so much for staking out the camera store for Walter!"

"Yeah, but maybe it's just as well. It might be too risky. If he sees us over on the island we might not get off."

We jumped on the 4:45 boat with the knowledge that there was something going on, and that something was more than just crazy Walter on the loose.

When we got off the boat, we headed straight down the street to the parking lot. Boom Boom wasn't on duty, but that didn't mean anything because he always hung out at the lot even when he wasn't on the clock. Mark and I both asked him if he wanted to go with us for an orange sherbet cooler, my treat. All I had to say was "my treat." We jumped in his old brown truck and headed for the ice cream store. We sat in a booth. Mark and I got a couple of sodas because we were a little tired of ice cream. Boom Boom told our waitress, Melissa, "The usual." The usual was an orange sherbet cooler with extra orange sherbet ice cream.

"OK, Orville, what is it?" he asked between sips of his cooler.

"What's what?" I was trying to ease my way into asking him about the pictures.

"I know you want to ask me something. Do you need time off already and you want me to cover? 'Cause I will, but I don't think Tommy will be too pleased."

"No, it's nothing about work. It's . . . you claim you know everything about Belltown's history."

"Claim? Orville, I don't claim anything. It's just a simple fact. I've spent seventy-something years in this town." He took another sip of his cooler.

"Well, we've got some pictures, and we were wondering if you knew who the people are."

Mark handed the pictures to Boom Boom, and he looked down at the picture of the woman and baby dancing cheek to cheek.

"Oh, Louise," he said softly. "She was so young and beautiful, so full of hopes and dreams."

"That's Louise Sherwin?" Mark interrupted.

"Yes. That's the lady who you kids called old lady Sherwin. She's not so old there is she, Orville?" Boom Boom looked over at me and waited for my answer. There was sincerity in his voice.

"No, she's not. She's beautiful!" I felt guilty that my friends and I had called this woman old lady Sherwin and had made up stories about her just to make our neighborhood more exciting.

"Did you know her . . . a long time ago?" I could tell Mark felt guilty, too, because of the hesitation in his voice.

"Well," Boom Boom took another sip, "she was much older than I was, but I knew her. When I was little, I was sweet on her, but every boy in Belltown was, and then . . . He stopped as he came to the picture of the mayor.

"Where did you get these pictures, Orville?" His soft voice was now loud and angry as he threw down the mayor's picture.

"I can't tell you that, Boom Boom. I'm sorry. I have to keep that secret. Who is that man?" I pointed to the picture of the mayor.

"I don't know! I gotta get going!" His tone was harsh, his manner all locked up. But Mark was going to take a stab at it.

"Do you know who the baby is?"

"No, I don't know, Mark. Thanks for the cooler, Orville. See you at work." Boom Boom stood up and walked out.

"I guess that means he's not going to give us a ride home." Mark tried to make light of Boom Boom's departure.

"Yeah. Wow! Did you see his reaction when he saw the mayor's picture?" I said as I pulled out my wallet to pay the check.

"It was obvious Boom Boom knew the guy. If we find out who the guy is, we'll probably find out why Walter wanted his picture and Miss Sherwin's, and maybe why he killed her."

That night, my head was entertaining a tennis match of thoughts about Maria and questions about the case. I kept thinking of Maria; I knew I either had to tell her how I felt by the end of the summer or just come to my senses and give it up. Questions about the case were driving me crazy.

What does Walter want with pictures of a long time ago? And who was the mayor? And why did Boom Boom hate him? They say a picture tells a thousand stories, or something like that. I just wanted it to tell one—what did all this have to do with Miss Sherwin's death?

Chapter
Five

THREE DAYS had passed since we got the pictures. Boom Boom never mentioned the pictures again. Mark and I were a little confused about how to continue our investigation, so we decided to visit Will and ask him. Mrs. Harris was thrilled to see us, but I told her that we wanted to spend time with just one patient. She bought my story that spending time with more than one patient would be a little overwhelming on our first visit. We told her how we had met Will and that we'd wanted to spend time with him. She agreed, saying, "Will could use the company; he's been very depressed lately."

Mark and I walked into Will's room and found him lying in bed. It was 3:00 in the afternoon, and he was in bed. Mark tried some humor, "Hey, Will, I've heard of oversleeping, but this is ridiculous."

"Yeah, rough night," I added.

Will managed a smile.

"I thought I'd never see you two guys again."

"Hey, we said we'd visit you, and here we are."

"Anyway, it's not every day that we can pick the brain of a PI."

I threw the envelope on his bed. He propped himself up and studied the pictures while I told him about the camera store and Boom Boom.

"Well, men, it's fairly logical how you can find out who the mayor is."

"How's that?" Mark asked.

"Just go to Town Hall. They must have old portraits hanging up there. Come on, men, you can do better than that."

He was right—that was a given. We both should have thought of it, but we didn't. In a way, it may have been a blessing in disguise that we didn't think of it. The change in Will's demeanor was promising, and our overlooking the obvious helped that change. We hung out with Will for about forty-five minutes and talked about ourselves. He never once mentioned his past, not even any old PI stories. We weren't going to force any, either. We left somewhat satisfied not only about the case but also about Will.

When I came home, Mom and Dad told me we were going to have a family meeting. My little brother, Billy, said right off, "Whatever it is, I didn't do it!"

"No one is in trouble. We just have some family news to discuss," my father reassured us.

We sat around the kitchen table and Dad poured some pink lemonade.

"Your mother has something to tell you," Dad continued, pouring into my sister Jackie's glass.

My mom started by saying, "I just came from Mr. Wood's office. Mr. Wood was Miss Sherwin's lawyer. Well, apparently, Miss Sherwin had a will drawn up last year.

Anyway, Miss Sherwin left our family a wonderful gift. She left us her home."

"What?" we all chorused.

"I know—I couldn't believe it, either. But Mr. Wood said that Miss Sherwin wanted her home to be in safe hands and she knew that she could trust the Jacques family." My mother had a huge smile on her face.

"See what happens if you're charitable," said my father. "Your mother was good to Miss Sherwin, and Miss Sherwin didn't forget that. Now, just so you know, it's not totally free. Miss Sherwin paid off her mortgage, but she took out a second mortgage on the house. We will pick that up. It's not that much. And your mother and I feel it is a great investment for you children."

Dad waited to field questions.

My mind drifted to the words "in safe hands." Safe from what? And why would an old woman have to remortgage her house? Why would she need that kind of money? I couldn't believe that we were going to own the house that had played such a big role in our neighborhood's folklore. I knew all my friends would be chomping at the bit to check out the scariest house in Belltown. Yes, I definitely was the man. My first guests in the house would have to be Mark and Maria. I knew Maria would want to see the house, and that would be an excuse to see her. Of course, it would be rather obvious if I didn't invite my best friend along. But more than these things, I realized that I would soon have unlimited access to the house, to search for clues.

By the time I got to the harbor that night, I think

everyone in Belltown had heard that the Jacques family was the new owner of Miss Sherwin's house. Joe Clancy and Geoff Myer ran over to me.

"Jedi, Jedi!" Joe called out as he waddled over.

"Hey, Orville," Geoff yelled.

"What do you guys want?" I asked, knowing the answer.

"So when are you gonna take us to see what the inside of the house looks like?" Geoff got right to the point.

"Yeah, Jedi, I bet there are dead bodies in the cellar. When are you gonna let us take a look?" Joe begged.

"First of all, before I open it as a museum and charge admission, I've got to see for myself what it looks like. Then maybe—just maybe—I'll let you guys take a look."

Their eyes widened.

"Can I take a tour, too, sometime?" A voice came from behind me. It was Maria. I turned slowly to face her. Her flowered sun dress danced from side to side with the harbor breeze.

"Ah, hey, Maria," I managed.

"Hi, Orville. Do you think I could take a look at Miss Sherwin's house sometime?" When you like someone, you tend to analyze every move she makes and every word she utters. My analysis concluded that she wanted to spend time with me. Do I do the smart thing and invite her to come over and take a look at the house? Yes.

"If, ah, you're not busy, Maria . . . would you like to come over tomorrow night?"

"It would be kind of scary, but it might be fun," she smiled.

"I mean, you can bring Mark with you."

"Oh ... OK. That would be fun. How about tomorrow night at eight?"

"Yeah, sounds good. See you later." I got on my bike and rode away, shaking my head. I couldn't believe how stupid I was. I kept mimicking my own voice. "I mean you can bring Mark." The girl of my dreams was going to come over and I was going to give her a tour of a haunted house. She would get scared, and I would tell her not to worry, and our eyes would meet and ... just like that—we'd kiss. But, good ol' Orville says, "I mean you can bring Mark." What an idiot you are, Orville, I thought as I rounded the corner and approached my house. Two cruisers flew past me and headed three houses up from Miss Sherwin's at Mr. Saires's house and parked there. An ambulance came barreling down the street. The neighbors gathered on Mr. Saires's lawn and watched and whispered, wondering what was going on. The paramedics brought Mr. Saires out on a stretcher; not a word had to be spoken. Mr. Saires, a seventy-five-year-old retiree from the Belltown fire department, was dead.

"How'd it happen?" everyone asked Sergeant Gonestone.

"Natural causes." He then ordered his troops to control the crowd.

"Who found him?" Geoff Myer asked, jumping off his bike.

"Yes, who found him?" Geoff's father said louder. He thought an older voice might get Gonestone's attention—perhaps even an answer. No such luck. Geoff's question raised an important issue. Mr. Saires lived alone. He was very unfriendly and kept to himself. So if he died of natural causes, who found him? Gonestone tried to ignore the questions, but the neighbors wanted answers. Finally, he let it slip out.

"All right, all right. We got a 911 call, saying a man was in trouble at this address. So it was probably Mr. Saires himself."

I spoke up, "If that was the case, wouldn't Mr. Saires have said, 'This is Mr. Saires. I need help!'?"

Everyone nodded in agreement. Gonestone shoved his pad in his back pocket and escaped to his cruiser. My neighbors were getting nervous. Two people were dead. Sure, they were old, and, yes, their deaths could have been due to natural causes or accidents, but now, it wasn't only Mark and I who wondered about murder!

The sign on the front door of Town Hall read Summer Hours: 7 AM—5:30 PM. It was now 6:38. In other words, the summer schedule was for the convenience of town officials who wanted to take an early evening swim or get in nine holes before dinner. Mark and I couldn't wait another day to find out the identity of our mystery mayor. We went around to the back of the building and looked for some way to get in. There was a window wide open on the second floor. All we had to do was climb on top of a dumpster, and we were level with the window. We were hardly scaling walls or shutting down security systems or anything. It took all of ten seconds to get in.

"Follow me. I know the room where they keep the portraits of all the town officials in. If our guy served here, his portrait will be in that room." Mark walked down the long corridor, and I followed.

"How do you know about the room?" I asked.

"You're not the only person on this case. I did a little P.I. work of my own last night. Custodians are a wealth of information."

I could tell he was trying not to smile. At the end of the corridor, we came to a room. Mark opened the door; his P.I. work had paid off. Inside the room was a round conference table surrounded by ten to fifteen portraits. It took us all of twenty seconds to find our man. It was just his face. He had the same stern, cold stare. We almost tripped over each other, running to get close enough to read his name.

"Mayor Wilson W. Sherwin." Mark emphasized each and every syllable.

"Wilson W. Sherwin," I repeated.

"That's Miss Sherwin's father, right?"

"Yeah, Mark. I never knew he was the mayor of Belltown. The rumor around town was he was overprotective of Miss Sherwin, but no one ever mentioned he was the mayor."

"I thought the story around town was that they lived off Miss Sherwin's great-grandfather's pirate money. I wonder why no one ever mentioned Wilson Sherwin was the mayor of Belltown."

"That's a nice way of saying I wonder why people kept it a secret."

"A secret," Mark said softly, nodding in agreement.

I broke down a bit and told my dad why I wanted to show Maria and Mark the Sherwin house. I said, "I want to impress them." He went into the other room and then came back with the key. I thanked him, and as I was walking out the door, he said, "Orville, since when did you ever want to impress Mark?" I broke a smile. My father knew there was only one person I wanted to impress.

I sat on the glider on Miss Sherwin's porch. It was rusty and squeaked as I swayed back and forth waiting for Mark and Maria. It probably hadn't been used in more than twenty years. I wondered if Miss Sherwin had sat on it with the baby. Was it her baby? What had happened to the baby? I also went over the town's story of Miss Sherwin. Did she really run away to be a vaudeville dancer? Did her father track her down and pour candle wax in her ears till her eardrums burst and yell "Dance to the sounds of silence!"? It would make sense that a pillar of the community would disapprove of his daughter's dancing back then, but would he do something that cruel? And why did the townsfolk leave out the fact that he was the mayor of Belltown when they told the story? Why was there never any mention of a Mrs. Sherwin? What happened to Miss Sherwin's mother? And why did Boom Boom hate Wilson

W. Sherwin? My mind was buzzing with questions, but it suddenly went blank when I saw Mark walk up the steps of the Sherwin porch.

"Where's Maria?" My heart was sinking. "Is she coming?"

"Yeah. She's right behind me." Mark eased onto the glider. "She's bringing a friend, if that's OK," Mark said nonchalantly.

I knew trouble when I heard it. Mark was going to send me down the river just so he could gain points with Maria.

"Who is it, Mark?"

"She's really cool, Orville."

I couldn't believe he started with that description.

"C'mon, Mark. This is Orville. Don't play with me like that. Who is it?"

"Ah, Sandra Vincent."

"Oh, my God! Sandra Vincent! Sandra Vincent!"

I couldn't believe it. Sandra Vincent brought board games to all the parties. She had arrived at Kim Archer's sweet-sixteen birthday party with Chutes and Ladders.

"I thought, Orville, since your luck isn't that great lately, we could show the girls the house and tell ghost stories and maybe, Sandra and you could—" Mark wasn't going to finish his sentence because I wasn't going to let him.

"Mark, don't do me any favors. First of all . . ."

I couldn't finish my sentence because Maria and Sandra showed up. There was nothing I could do but put up with it. My blood was boiling. Mark had talked down to me as if I couldn't find a girl. I had found the girl. That wasn't the problem. The problem was he took the girl I had found. And now he was talking to me, acting really smug, as if he was going to help me out. Some help!

"Hi, Orville!" Maria said.

"Hi, Maria! Hi, Sandy!" I was determined to make the best of it.

"It's Sandra. And hi, Orville!" Sandra walked up the steps, acting high and mighty. She was holding a couple of boxes.

"What did you bring, SANDRA?" I stressed her name.

"Well, I thought we could play some games, so I brought Connect Four, a Ouija board, and Operation . . ."

"The Milton Bradley game." I finished her sentence.

"Yes!" she beamed. "Do you like Operation, Orville?"

"I did in the second grade. Let's go into the house."

"Have you been in it yet?" Maria looked into my eyes.

"No. I haven't. I was tempted, but I figured I'd wait for you guys. My parents started cleaning it up today. They say it has a lot of potential."

There was a stairway facing us right where we walked in. I turned on the lights for the hallway and stairwell. At the top of the stairs, we could see the open bathroom door.

"Was that the bathroom where it . . ." Maria didn't know how to ask the question that was going through everybody's minds.

"Yes, my dad said it happened in the upstairs bathroom. So that must be it." We all hesitated at the stairwell.

"Why don't we check out the first floor and save the

second floor for later?" I suggested.

"Yeah, much later," Mark laughed.

There were five rooms on the first floor: the kitchen with a connecting pantry, the living room that had sliding doors to the den, and the dining room. I think we were expecting creaking sounds and cobwebs and dust on everything. If it weren't for the house's creepy past, it would've seemed just hushed and sad, but all right. Of course, none of us was going to go upstairs. So we wandered around the five rooms, checking out the antiques and old books.

After about fifteen minutes of snooping around the house, we settled in the den. Maria sat on the floor next to Mark and Sandra next to me on the couch. I wasn't pleased with the arrangement.

"It's funny how many stories have been told about this house. I was expecting a dungeon." Mark stretched and put his arm around Maria.

"It's actually really pretty," Maria agreed and accepted Mark's arm. The mood in the room was awkward; it reeked of a "We're a couple, you two aren't" atmosphere. Sandra was moving closer to me, and I was feeling sick, and it definitely wasn't the "good sick."

"So, do you want to play a game, Orville?" she whispered in my ear.

Good idea, I thought; but not the game Sandra had in mind. I spoke up and tried to interrupt the Velcro twins, who were now kissing. "Hey, you guys, Sandra wants to play a game." Maria and Mark stopped their kissing and looked up.

"How about Connect Four?" I offered.

"That's not the kind of game I meant." Sandra hung on my shoulder.

Mark and Maria went back to work, both assuming that I got Sandra's hint. I understood her hint all right, so I said out of desperation, "How about seeing if this house has any spirits?"

They both stopped and looked at me, intrigued. "What do you mean, Orville?" Mark asked.

"Well, Sandra, you brought a Ouija board, right?"

"Yeah." She answered.

"So, why don't we try to contact some spirits?"

"Yeah, that would be a blast," Mark agreed.

I wanted to use the Ouija board to kill some time. Mark wanted to use it for a different reason—to frighten Maria and then act like her protector. Sandra took the board out of the box while I turned the lights off and lit two candles to set the mood. Maria wanted to lead the group in the questioning; there was no way I was going to object. All four of us placed our fingertips lightly on the board.

"Hello, Ouija. We need your help tonight. We are trying to locate someone who has passed from this world. Will you help? Yes or No?"

Our fingers danced across the board to the word Yes.

Maria asked the group, "Who do you guys want to talk to?"

Sandra suggested, "How about Elvis?"

"Do you know how many Ouija boards are trying to contact Elvis?" Mark said to her, annoyed. "How about Stevie Ray Vaughan?"

"No, I hated his music," Sandra fought back. Mark and I rolled our eyes.

"Maria, how about asking Ouija to let us talk to who-ever wants to talk?" I said softly.

Maria didn't reply, she just went into her questioning.

"Ouija, is there anyone who wants to talk to us?"

It danced over the word Yes.

"We will talk. What is your name, spirit?"

The Ouija moved slowly as we said the letters softly and in unison. "L-o-u-i-s-e."

"Louise."

"Are you pushing it, Orville?" Mark asked, his voice quivering.

"I wouldn't joke about that, man." I kept my eyes focused on the board. We all did.

"Who is Louise, you guys?" Maria asked us.

"Let me do the questioning, Maria," I pleaded.

"OK whatever."

"Louise, is your last name Sherwin?" I asked.

The Ouija glided over to Yes.

"This isn't funny, you guys," Sandra squeaked.

"She's right. Maybe we'd better stop," Maria agreed.

"No, we have to keep going," I raised my voice. I knew that Mark wouldn't fool around when it came to Miss Sherwin, and I knew that the girls probably didn't even know her first name.

"Louise, this is your neighbor, Orville Jacques."

The Ouija started to move to the letters H and I.

"Hi. Oh, and hi to you, Louise. Louise, why do you want to talk to us?"

The Ouija slid to a stop on H, rested a couple of seconds and continued to E and did the same procedure for L and P. "H-E-L-P!", the four of us silently chanted. The group was now feeling extremely uneasy, including me, but I continued.

"Why do you need help?"

She spelled out the word, Dead.

"OK I don't quite understand dead. We know you're dead. Could you help us out a little?"

There was no reply.

"Orville, ask her how she died ," Mark suggested.

"We know how she died." Sandra added her two cents.

I was about to take Mark's advice when the Ouija started to move to the letter M. It stopped and then raced over to U, R, D, E, R.

"Murder."

At this point we all wanted out, but I had to continue. I don't know if I believed the board, but I didn't disbelieve, either.

"Louise, you were murdered. Did the man who escaped from the hospital murder you? His name was Walter."

The Ouija was quiet, but then started to move. I didn't know where the Ouija was going because the candles I had lit suddenly went out and the room was in complete darkness. The girls let out a scream. Let's face it, we all screamed and felt our way to the hall light. I turned it on and all four of us ran out of the house.

Sandra was yelling at Mark, saying he blew out the candles. But Mark couldn't have blown out all the candles—one of the candles was across the room, and the candles went out simultaneously. We went to the beach to sit and figure out what had just happened. Sandra's theory was that we set the whole thing up. Maria didn't know what to believe, and Mark and I knew more than we could tell either one. After about an hour, the girls went home. Mark and I sat on the beach wall and talked, convinced it was Louise Sherwin who had been communicating with us. We both thought we were silly to believe something coming from a board game that anyone could buy at any toy store. But we still believed that Miss Sherwin needed our help.

Chapter Six

THE NEXT MORNING, Mark came by the parking lot with coffee and donuts and the *Belltown News*. The coffee and donuts were his way of saying he was sorry. I didn't like coffee, but I drank it anyway because it made me feel older.

The *Belltown News* reported that Mr. Saires had died of natural causes, but there was no mention of the 911 call that Gonestone let slip out. Mr. Saires could have made that call, but Mark and I knew better. It didn't surprise me to read that Walter had been spotted in our neighborhood again. What I didn't understand was if someone witnessed Walter trying to kill Mr. Saires, why didn't that person come forward? I knew Gonestone didn't mention the 911 call in his comments to the paper. Deep down, the sergeant knew he couldn't handle a murder investigation. Mark and I talked for about fifteen minutes. Boom Boom said he could handle selling the parking tickets. It was unusually slow because the weather people predicted rain all day. So far, they were wrong. But predicting the weather in New England is about as safe as pitching a southpaw at Fenway Park!

"So, do we search Miss Sherwin's house today?" Mark asked.

"I can't today. I have to help my parents clean it. And move furniture about a thousand times." I was tired just thinking about it.

"Why? Are they going to try and rent it?" Mark quizzed.

"No. My mom is going to start a tutoring center."

"Oh, really? That's great. But can she do that right out of the house?"

"Oh yeah. She found out that Miss Sherwin's land is zoned for business, so she's pretty psyched. I'll keep my eyes open, but tomorrow we should really check the house."

"Yeah, it's a plan. Orville . . ." Mark paused.

I could see he was trying to think of the right words.

"Do you want to go to the county fair tonight?"

"Yeah, that would be a blast," I said.

"OK, it would be me, you and Maria and her cousin . . . Susan," the name hung in his throat.

"Susan? Who's Susan?"

"To tell you the truth, I don't know what she looks like. But, could you help me out? I'm sorry about last night. We'll have fun."

"I don't know." I pondered the idea of seeing Maria again.

"I understand why you wouldn't want to go, but Maria asked me when I saw her this morning to ask you." He looked at me desperately. But he didn't have to say another word. Maria wanted me to go, and that was all there was to it. If Maria wanted my company, even if I had to be with her cousin, I would go.

"OK," I said.

"She's Maria's cousin. She can't be that bad. She'll come by at 7:30," Mark smiled.

He had a point. But I didn't care what she looked like as long as I was going to be with Maria again.

Why wasn't I shocked when Sandra Vincent knocked on my door at 7:30 and told me that Susan couldn't make it? It's just my luck when it comes to the opposite sex. Sandra drove because she was the only one who had her license. We picked up Mark at his house, and I had every intention of throwing him the evil eye, but I could tell he was just as shocked to see Sandra as I was. We had to pick up Maria at work. She was a chambermaid at Mr. Anderson's motel. She also worked the front desk.

The Belltown County Fair goes on for nine days every summer. I never got tired of this fair; it always held an aura of magic and mystery. It was also the one time I could indulge in the types of foods every kid dreams of—cotton candy, candied apples, snow cones, fried dough, pizza, onion rings, and twirly fries. I get hungry just thinking about it! Of course, the first person we saw was the connoisseur of junk food—Joe Clancy. He ran up to us, with a snow cone in one hand and fried dough in the other one.

"Hey, Jedis, isn't this great?" His mouth was blue from the snow cone.

"Yeah, we just got here. What should we check out?" Mark asked.

"Well, there's the guys who ride motorcycles in the pit. That's pretty cool. And there's a woman who looks in a crystal ball, that was really cool 'cause she told me that I'd own a video arcade and an ice-cream store when I get old." Joe licked his snow cone and then took a bite from his fried dough.

"Can we go to the crystal-ball woman?" Maria asked.

"Yeah, sure." I answered for Mark.

"Wow, chili dogs!" Joe pointed his cone in the direction of the chili dog stand. "Later, Jedis."

"Yeah, later, Joe."

There was no line in front of Hilda's Amazing Crystal Ball. Hilda lived in an old painted wagon. The man selling the tickets said that one person could go in at a time. Maria went in first. She was only in there for about five minutes; and when she came out, she wouldn't tell us anything about the woman or what she had seen in the ball. I went in next. Hilda was an old woman dressed in what looked like a thousand scarves, sitting at a table. Her mouth was covered with a silk handkerchief. I could tell she was old by her hands and her voice: Her hands were wrinkled sticks; her voice was tired and brittle and she had a foreign accent.

"Sit down, young man," she managed. She sounded as if this was a chore.

"Vhat is your name, son?" She put her hands on the crystal ball.

"My name is Orville, Orville Jacques." I tried to get comfortable in my chair.

"Orville, a strange name. Let me see if you have a strange future."

She looked in the ball for about a minute, and my curiosity made me move in closer to take a closer look for myself. As I moved my body forward my leg accidentally brushed against her leg.

"Sorry," I said.

"Zat is all right," She waved her hand as she continued to stare into the ball, but then the passive expression on her face changed to shock and then clouded, "Oh, Orville! Zere are zings you have been keeping secret. You have been keeping zem secret for your safety. Is zat true?" She was now interested in me, and what she was saying blew me away.

"Yes, it's true. What else are you seeing?" I lunged forward.

As she peered into the ball, I kept my eyes fixed on her expression. Her eyes widened and her eyebrows arched.

"What do you see?"

"Ahm . . . you vill have a nice life."

I could tell that she was making this up.

"Come on, what do you see?" I begged.

"I vill tell you zis much and no more. Our secrets are our sickness. You, my son, will not be secret for long, and you vill unlock many secrets. Now, you must go."

She pointed to the door.

I was going to ask for more information when she raised her hand and said, "Stop! No more! Except, never overlook."

"Overlook what?"

"You know."

"The obvious." I said it almost as if I was talking to myself.

She winked and waved me on my way.

I walked out of there just a little spooked; after the Ouija board incident, there wasn't much that could surprise me.

"What'd she say?" Mark asked.

"It's a secret. Let's go to the bumper cars," I suggested. We rode the bumper cars, the Ferris wheel, the Sky Diver, the whole nine yards. Everyone was having a blast— everyone except me. I went through the motions but I couldn't get my mind off the fortune-teller woman. This supernatural stuff was just too weird. I knew I had to find Walter before he found me. He had the advantage—he knew where I lived!

After the fair, Sandra suggested we go to The Bump. The Bump was like an island because it stuck out into the ocean. To get to The Bump, you had to walk down a long path in the woods. I didn't want to go because people usually went to The Bump to do one thing—kiss. Of course, our only light was the moon, and that was about as helpful as a bathroom night light. When we were halfway there, a flock of sea gulls screamed above us. I felt a hand grab mine. I couldn't even see in front of me, so I figured it was Sandra, but then the voice said, "Oh, sorry, Orville. I got a little scared." It was Maria. The realization then hit me. Her hand was in my hand. For one brief moment, we were hand in hand. It was a wonderful feeling. Then Mark's voice brought me back to earth.

"Hey, keep your hands off my girl," he said, in mock anger.

"My girl!" The words ripped at my heart and I thought, for a best friend, I don't like Mark that much right now. It was my blind jealously that was doing the thinking. We trudged down the path, pushing the hanging branches out of the way. We finally came out of the woods, and the ocean that had been calling us was there beyond the clearing known as The Bump. The moon was more generous to The Bump than it had been to the path in the woods. It was truly a breathtaking sight: the moon shimmering on the lapping waves as the silhouetted sea gulls dived beneath for some late-night snacks. I really could see how the view from The Bump could put anyone in the mood.

"You guys, I gotta get going."

"Oh, don't leave, Orville. We just got here," said Maria.

Not even Maria could persuade me to stay a second longer.

"No, I feel pretty sick. It must've been all that junk food from the fair."

"Well, I can give you a ride home." Sandra just didn't get it. In a way, I was glad she didn't get it because I really didn't want to hurt her feelings. I know you probably don't believe me but it's true, maybe I felt that way because I knew that feeling of rejection.

"No, thanks. I think the walk will be good for me."

"Yeah, Orville, walk home and you'll probably feel better from the fresh air," Mark added. He knew Sandra was going to third-wheel it, but he owed more than coffee and donuts this time. I walked away from them having the same feeling I get when I go to the nurse's office to avoid taking a test—unquestionable relief. Of course, now I was walking alone along a dark path! I could hear a couple of raccoons or possums arguing behind me so I picked up the pace. The trees and bushes kept rustling, and I started to think myself into fright. I tried not to think of the case but the harder I tried, the more I thought and the faster I walked. Halfway down the path, it began to sprinkle. The wind picked up, and I was suddenly shelled by a downpour. I began to jog cautiously through the darkness. I couldn't help but think of Ouija boards, fortune-tellers, Miss Sherwin's finger pointing, and most of all, crazy Walter. I felt I was being chased. My mind was playing tricks on me, and I was falling for all of them. Frantically pushing branches aside, I started a full sprint. It was then that the thunder and lightning kicked in.

The thunder boomed, adding to the ominous atmosphere. The lightning actually guided me as it lit up the path about every fifteen seconds, though I still managed to fall a couple of times. After I fell down the third time, I yelled at myself, "C'mon, Orville! Grow up! This is ridiculous, being scared of nothing." I found a dry spot on my shirt and wipe the rain off my glasses. I stopped running and broke into a brisk walk. The wind whipped along, whistling through the woods and planting the sea's salt spray along the path. The lightning flashed like a camera.

Each time it flashed I saw bits of landscape. The trees and bushes appeared as clothes hanging like figures in a closet. The lightning kept reassuring me that these weren't the feared monster.

When the lightning flashed again, what I saw in front of me didn't bend back like trees. It looked like a person on all fours. But just as I was piecing it all together, the path was black again. The adrenaline started to pump and jump. Do I wait for the lightning to see or jump into the bushes? Curiosity was going to kill me. The path lit up again. I still couldn't make it out, but I could tell it was coming closer. I braced myself as I kept my eyes on the black path. The light finally came. It was right in front of me. I screamed until it answered with a bark. Yes, a bark. I put my hand out and a happy, slobbering golden retriever began licking away.

I let out a laugh and petted the dog. I had nearly driven myself crazy! After a couple of seconds, the dog took off back down the path from where he had come. The thunder and lightning never let up, but I was almost at the end of the path when I heard a group of screams. It must be the girls and Mark, I thought. They sounded only about a hundred yards away. I was now relaxed and figured I'd wait and give them a good scare. The lightning kept flashing. I thought I saw something, but I realized it must be the dog, so I called him. "Come here, boy. Come here, boy." I put my hand out and waited for the flash.

The flash came—and lit up Walter's face. He was not even five feet away. Walter stood before me, this time wearing a sick, twisted smile as he ssshhh-ed me with his fingers on his lips. I knew then why characters don't move in horror movies—they can't! I couldn't move at all. The sight of Walter's smile drained all my energy. I was in shock.

Finally he moved toward me saying something that was muffled by the thunder. He lit up and went dark again. As soon as he went dark, I was able to turn and move my legs, which had felt like lead weights. But once I got in running motion, my adrenaline kicked into overdrive, and I took off. I could hear voices in front of me. They weren't far away. I ran toward the voices, but I really couldn't tell where I was going. My rain-stained glasses were fogging up; I quickly became completely blind. The voices were closer, but I couldn't open my mouth to call out to them. But I could hear the ominous sound of Walter's feet splashing. I was lost in a labyrinth of wiry brush, all I could do was hear. I heard the waves crashing against the jetties. I heard the wind. But what I heard most clearly was my panting and his panting, until they were one. Then I didn't hear anything.

I woke up to an old woman's face looking down at me. I couldn't make out her face too clearly because I didn't have my glasses. I could see that there was something wrong with her left eye. It was abnormal. It sagged down. It sagged down as far as her left cheekbone. I was too tired to react to the eye. My head felt like a battle zone, and I could hardly keep my eyes open.

"How are you feeling, Orville?" she smiled down.

"Where am I?""Who are you?""And how do you know my name?"The questions took a few seconds to get out.

"You're in my guest room. My name is Martha Halloran. And how do I know your name? Walter told me." She started to pour me a cup of tea.

"Walter! You mean crazy Walter?" I pushed the covers off me. She let out a warm giggle as she tried to hand me the cup of tea.

"Walter's not crazy. He's just a little misunderstood. Here, have your tea."

"I'm sorry. But the guy just tried to kill me. He's not misunderstood. He's crazy." I balked at the tea and rose to get out of the bed.

"You see, Orville, that's a perfect example of Walter being misunderstood. He told me he was trying to talk to you and you ran away from him."

She took my glasses out of her apron and handed them to me.

"No offense. But if an escaped mental patient met you face to face in the woods, would you wait to stop and chat?" I put my glasses on and saw her deformity defined much more clearly; but because of her laid-back manner, I didn't freak out.

"Good point," she said with a laugh, but then her tone became serious. "Walter needs your help."

"My help? I can't help him." I was frustrated and confused.

"Why? 'Cause he escaped from a hospital?" she asked.

"No, 'cause he's a kill ..." I stopped.

"A killer. Walter told me that you think he killed Louise. Walter didn't kill Louise. He loved her. He wanted to protect her again."

Again? The word slipped out of her mouth, and I jumped all over it.

"Again? What do you mean, again?" I was now intrigued and in no hurry to leave, so I picked up the tea and sipped some. Martha was visibly working out the right words in her head. She ignored my question.

"Why don't I let Walter tell you why he needs your help."

Martha Halloran got up, went to the bedroom door, and slowly opened it. Walter stood there. As I looked at him, I trembled, spilling the tea on the blankets. I put the cup on the counter and nervously wiped the blankets with my shirt.

"I, ah," Walter paused, "I didn't mean to scare you back there on the path."

There was sincerity in his voice, but I didn't answer him. I was still petrified at seeing him in the flesh, and so close.

"It's ah . . . I just didn't know how to talk to you," he said, moving closer to the bed.

Finally, I managed to speak. "Well, how did I get this bump on my head? Did you hit me?"

"No. I didn't hit you. You started to run, and then you fell and bumped your head. I didn't know what to do."

Martha spoke up. "So Walter carried you here. I live about a quarter of a mile from The Bump."

She came over and began to clean the tea stain off

the blankets. Walter looked almost childlike. I could tell he genuinely felt sorry for scaring me. I was now a little more comfortable in his presence, but I still had to be cautious. I mean, I didn't know this Halloran woman. She could be a wacko, too. One question would tell me what these people were after.

"What do you want from me, Walter?"

Walter looked over at Martha for approval, and she nodded her head.

"Well, I know you think I killed my mother, but I didn't."

"Your mother!" I shouted.

"Yes. Louise Sherwin was my mother. I loved her, and I would never have hurt her. You've got to believe me."

Pieces of the puzzle were beginning to fit. The little baby in the pictures was Walter. But why had Walter come out of hiding to ask me to believe him?

"You see, I got this note from Mother, so I escaped," he said. I took the paper from Walter, and read it to myself:

My dear Walter,

I need your help. I know he is watching me. He has killed before. He will kill again. I think I'm next. Please come quick, son. I know the police won't believe me.

Sincerely,

Mother

"I thought Miss Sherwin didn't have any children?" I directed the question to Walter. Walter hung his head and walked out of the room. Martha yelled to him. "Walter!

Walter! Please come back here and finish talking to Orville."

She then turned to me.

"You see, Orville, Walter was an illegitimate child. He was born in a time when that was so frowned upon that Louise never told anyone she had had him. She kept him in the house, and he was never allowed to go outside or even look out the windows. But he never stopped loving his mother, and he often protected her."

"From what?"

"Well," she paused, and again I could tell she was choosing her words carefully, "Miss Sherwin's father was very upset that she had an illegitimate child, so whenever he drank, he beat her. Walter would always step in front of his mother and take the beating. That's why he has so many scars on his back."

I wanted to find out more about Walter's past, but Martha decided she had said enough, or maybe, too much.

"So, Orville, from the note Walter received, it looks as if Louise was murdered. But Walter can't go to the police—who would believe him?"

I nodded.

"He's been watching you and your friend, and he thinks you could help him."

I played devil's advocate. "Well, what if Miss Sherwin was just a little paranoid, and she really did fall?"

"I thought that was the case until Walter heard Mr. Saires yell for help the other night. He saw Mr. Saires struggling with another man."

"So he called 911."

"Yes," her eyes widened.

"Could he describe the other man?"

"No, he just saw two shadows and heard the yelling. Orville, Mr. Saires didn't have a heart attack. He was murdered."

I recorded every word that Walter and Martha Halloran had told me. I was blown away by this new information. I felt relieved that Walter wasn't going to be stalking me anymore, but I was back to square one. Or was I?

Chapter Seven

I KNEW IT WAS late when I saw my house in darkness. I sneaked in through the back door, expecting to be greeted by frowning parents or Ophelia's barking. Neither happened. Ophelia snored away and then growled a little, probably dreaming about chasing rabbits, I thought. The kitchen clock informed it was 2:37 AM. "I'm busted," I whispered to myself. I slithered up the stairs and put my ear against my parents' door. It sounded as if they were having the same dream as Ophelia! Maybe I'll get away with it, I thought. I fell into my bed and lay there for about an hour. I was beyond tired, but I couldn't stop thinking about Walter and Miss Halloran. I was now more interested in Walter's past than in the case. Questions I should've asked were now banging in my brain. How did Walter know he could go to Miss Halloran? How did Miss Halloran know so much about Walter's past? Who was Miss Halloran? Why did Walter want my help? I agreed to help him, but what could I really do? I had to go see Will and ask for his advice. He would know what to do. Deep down, I did believe Miss Halloran and Walter. There was a killer in

Belltown, and I had to find out who it was before it was too late.The strange thing was, as my eyes got heavy,I was not thinking of possible suspects. I was thinking about Walter's past.Then my heavy eyes got heavier.

My mom tugged at my covers."Rise and shine!"

"Rise and shine? It's 8:30, and it's my day off." I protested.

"I know it's your day off, but you're going to help me clean Miss Sherwin's house. Now, rise and shine!"

My mom shut the door before I could plead my case. I dragged my body out of bed, my head still throbbing. I decided I wouldn't fight my mother. I would do all the chores she wanted, and then I'd go and see Will. I knew he'd steer me in the right direction.

My mother gave me a list of chores that would make Cinderella look underworked.I wasn't pleased, but I didn't let it show. I just nodded and put the list into my back pocket. I had to wash floors, take down pictures, move furniture around, bring in books and put up shelves for the books.These were just a few things, but when I'm not getting paid, it's hard for me to be motivated. Music is the only thing that keeps me going when I get roped into family chores, so I put on my Walkman and turned the dial to 98.5 WBMX.

"Coming up, a block of U2," D.J.John Lander said.That would make scrubbing floors tolerable,I thought. I got on my hands and knees and began to scrub the wooden pantry floor. I scrubbed to "Party Girl" and half of "Walk On." The cloth snagged on one of the floorboards so I stopped scrubbing. I pulled at the cloth but part of it had dug into a crack in the board. I tugged harder and the cloth came out, but also loosened the floorboard. It seemed a little too loose; I couldn't have done that, I thought. I went into the kitchen and got a screwdriver out of the toolbox. I fiddled with the loose floorboard for a couple of minutes until the board was ready to be removed. Ironically, as I removed the board, "I Still Haven't Found What I'm Looking For" kicked in on my headset. Right under the floor was an object, a box or something. I loosened the other board, and I could see a small tin box. I turned off my Walkman and grabbed the box. "Maybe it's Miss Sherwin's lost treasure map," I thought. Nervous excitement was coursing through my body. I tried to open the box, but I quickly realized it was locked. I studied the lock and saw it was meant for a small key. I checked my pockets for the keys to Miss Sherwin's house. The ring held five keys, all the same size except for one—a small jagged key. Maybe this was it? I sighed and turned the key. The lock clicked—the box opened! There was no treasure map inside, just a few pieces of paper with the same handwriting I had seen the night before, Miss Sherwin's handwriting. The papers looked as though they had been pulled out of a journal. It read:

To Whom It May Concern:
My name is Louise W. Sherwin and I've lived in this house for eighty-plus years. The following is a confession, for I feel I may go to the grave having never spoken my secrets, but it is my desire to leave this world with the truth known.

I have not spoken the truth for all these years out of fear and shame. I believed I was honoring my name, but I was honoring a lie. I should keep silent and not destroy my family name. My great-great-grandfather tarnished the name long before me. He was a pirate, who made his living murdering and robbing the innocent. Years later, my father, Wilson W. Sherwin, continued the tradition of feeding off the innocent. I stayed silent. I will no longer stay silent!

My father was the well-respected mayor of Belltown, who so eloquently spoke as a leader. He referred to the residents of Belltown as his people. He was trusted. When he came home, though, the devil controlled his tongue. He would keep a bottle of whiskey in one hand and a paddle in the other. He beat my mother until either she or he passed out. When I was ten, my mother disappeared. My father said that she left because I wasn't a good girl. No one knew where she went. I knew better, but I kept silent. My father told me, "You are now the Lady of the house. You have to act like a grown-up." So he made me act like a grown-up. I couldn't play or dance or listen to music. So whenever my father went to work or to drink or to do both, I would put the radio on and sing and dance to the big bands. I had a dream to run away and become a vaudeville dancer, so I never spent one dime of the money I got for Christmas and birthday gifts from my aunts, or the money I made sewing for my neighbors. I saved it all. The day finally came when I was sixteen. I ran away. I auditioned to be a dancer and I was chosen as an alternate. That meant I learned the routines and would go on if one of the dancers was sick. The manager gave me a job as cigarette girl so I could have an income. My father and Belltown were a faraway memory. I was beginning a new life. I fell in love with one of the dancers, Anthony Grange. We planned on getting married. That was the happiest six months of my life. Then one night after a show, Anthony and I were walking in the parking lot toward his car. We stopped at the car and he gave me a tender kiss. His love warmed my whole body. A voice interrupted our kissing—a familiar voice. A man, a few cars down, shouted that he had car trouble. Anthony went over to help him, and then I saw him struggle with the man. I ran over to see what was going on. When I got close enough, I saw it was my father. He was beating Anthony with a tire iron. I screamed and tried to make him stop, and then he hit me until I was unconscious. I awoke back in Belltown.

I had lost my hearing from the beating. He locked me in my room for months, so he was unable to notice the change taking place in my body. One day, I was able to sneak out and send a letter to Anthony. I got the letter back in the mail before my father saw it. It read "Deceased. Return to sender." I knew how he had died, but I kept silent about it. About three months after that, my hearing came back. I didn't tell anyone I could hear. I didn't tell because it was easier to hide from my father when he thought I couldn't hear. It pains me to state the obvious if you haven't understood why I hid. It was not just because he beat me. It was why. He was ashamed of me because I had a child out of wedlock. Back then, I thought it was my fault. I thought that I wasn't a good person. I wish society was as educated then as it is today. Maybe I wouldn't have kept Anthony's child a secret. Maybe my cousin Martha wouldn't have either, when my father ripped her eye with a broken whiskey bottle and called her a sinner. He caught her kissing a man good night at my aunt's house. He called my cousins and me his children. He was right. We all were. He tried so desperately to control all of our lives. He forbade me and my cousins Martha Halloran, Ben "Boom Boom," Betsey and Margaret Samuelson to ever date or marry. He had total control over all our lives. That is why he became insane when I had Walter. My father forced me to keep him a secret. I was a disgrace to the family name. That is what I'm most sorry for. I believed it. That is why Walter never had a chance to develop into a normal boy. He never stopped protecting me, though. My father was beating me one night and Walter couldn't take it anymore. He grabbed the paddle and beat my father to death. We buried my father where I knew my mother was buried—in the dirt cellar. Walter poured cement in the cellar floor. I told everyone that my father disappeared. I think everyone knew, but they kept it secret and only bits of the story have come out over the years about me. I am not sorry I helped get rid of a man who used power to steal from the innocent. He stole everything that was dear to me. I had to put Walter in a home because he was mentally abused for years and there was no way I could manage him. The pirate money has paid for that, but that has run out. I now have to

*remortgage the house. If not, I don't know what I'll do,
but that will be history when this is found. I have one
major regret in my life—keeping secrets. Do what you
want with this confession, but learn this much from it.
Our secrets are our sickness; indeed, they have made of
my life one long disease.*

My hands trembled as I put the pieces of paper back
into the box and shut it. I was shaking for several reasons.
For one, most of my questions were now answered. But it
was the way they had been answered that frightened me.
What were the chances of my snagging a piece of cloth
on the floorboard? Very slim—but it had happened. Did a
force greater than I could ever imagine make it happen? I
don't know, but I did know I was becoming more open-
minded when it came to the supernatural. I had heard the
phrase, "Our secrets are our sickness" before. I kept saying
it over and over and then a picture came into my mind. I
pictured the fortune-teller saying those words to me. What
else did she say? I thought for a moment. "You vill unlock
many secrets." The words flowed out of my mouth.

"Oh, my God!" I exclaimed. I grabbed the box and
made my way back to the comforts of my own house.
Once I was in my room, I opened the box and read the
confession again. The fortune-teller was right on target. I
had unlocked many secrets of Belltown's history: I now
knew what happened to Louise Sherwin's mother, why

no one mentioned Mr. Sherwin was mayor. They didn't want to taint Belltown's image. I knew the answers to why Boom Boom had become so enraged when he saw Mr. Sherwin's picture; what Martha Halloran's connection with Walter was, and how her eye became so deformed; and what had happened to Mr. Sherwin. All the pieces of the past now fit. Now what? I knew the truth, but what real purpose would it serve to make the truth known? The damage had already been done; the victims could no longer benefit.

I had to go see Will and ask his advice. He could help me figure out what to do with all this information. There was also a more important reason why I had to see him— there was still a killer on the loose. There was no time to finish my chores, and there was no time to call Mark.

I jumped on my mountain bike and headed for Bayside. The only hint of light in Will's room peeked through the crack in the curtains. Will was lying in bed, staring at the ceiling. My heart hit the floor. I knew the only reason he was still in bed on this sunny afternoon on the Cape was depression. I took a deep breath before I entered the room. I'm not a psychologist, so I was trying to think of the best way to approach the scene. I wish Mark were here, I said to myself. At least we were able to play off each other, but I was on my own, and I decided I'd act upbeat and then just go by my own instincts.

"Hey, Will! It's me, Orville." I walked over to the curtains and pulled the cord to open them.

"What do you want?" He put his arms in front of his face, shielding the glaring sun.

"What do I want? I want your help." I was faking a smile, but I really didn't feel like smiling. The atmosphere was making me depressed, too.

"Can't you see I'm trying to sleep here!" He put his arms down and pointed to the door. He gave me a long glare to scare me out of there. I wasn't going to budge. I let my instincts take over.

"I need your help, Will."

"I can't help you. I couldn't help . . . I can't help anybody," he managed, eyes watering.

"I need your help, Will, and I really have no time for you feeling sorry for yourself."

"Well, that's a heck of a thing to say to someone who is depressed," he said, offended.

"Let's face it! I'm just a kid. I don't know how to approach you. And I'm not a doctor. So, I'm not going to tiptoe around your feelings. You can lie here all day and feel sorry for yourself for all I care."

"Good! 'Cause I can't help you." His eyes were now completely filled as he pulled the covers over himself I turned to leave, but then I stopped at the door.

"Remember this, Will. We know you as a friend. Friends help friends, but if you can't help me, well . . ." I looked at him long and hard as he ignored me and stared straight up at the ceiling.

As I turned and shut the door behind me, I heard him

yell my name. I opened the door; he was propped up in his bed, giving me the same sorrowful look.

"Yeah, what, Will?"

"You're right, Orville. But you didn't have to give me that 'After School Special' attitude!" Will smiled, and we both chuckled.

"Now, how can I help you?" He scratched his beard. For the next half-hour, I filled him in on everything that had happened. Retelling the story, I realized I had quite an adventure and I still didn't have the killer. Will nodded and didn't show any signs of shock as I told my story, not even at the supernatural stuff. He probably had seen it all when he was a P.I., I thought.

"So, how can I help you?"

"Well, I've got three questions. Do I make Miss Sherwin's past public? And if Walter isn't the killer, who is? And where do I begin to figure it out?"

"Question number one, what do you think, Orville?"

"Well, who really benefits from the knowledge? If Walter finds out the truth of what happened to his father, he might become worse. Mr. Sherwin has already damaged him enough."

"Correct. The only person who would benefit would be YOU, and I don't think you're the type to cash in on other people's pain. But then again, it is a part of Belltown history, and it would explain a lot about some of the townspeople's lives in Belltown. If I were you, I would make it public, but only after all the victims have died. History does teach."

Will had a point. I never would have considered making it public, but it would clear up the misconceptions that some of the townsfolk had of Miss Sherwin. In time, I would make it public record.

"Now, I can't answer question two, Orville. I can say that you have already cleared up some mysteries of this town. I wouldn't be surprised if you found the answer to the second question very soon."

"Yeah, but I cleared up those mysteries out of luck. If I didn't find the confession, I probably never . . ."

"But you did find the confession. And that's why you'll find the killer, because you're nosey and lucky. The best PI's are both those things. Also, you don't disregard any information." Will was speaking quickly. This subject was his thing, and I could tell he was coming alive talking about it.

"What do you mean, I don't 'disregard any information'?"

"The fortune teller. Most people would have laughed at her predictions and forgot about them five minutes later. You didn't laugh. You remembered what she said. I had a case once where a psychic was predicting where people would be murdered. It took five murders before anyone listened to her." Will smiled.

"But what do I do now?"

"You stay curious, and the clues will come. Where's Mark, anyway?"

"He's probably out with his girlfriend." The last word pained me.

"I like Mark, Orville. But you might want to try to go solo on the rest of this mission."

"Why's that?"

"He'll end up telling her, and you don't need another person involved."

"Well, I'll think about it."

"It's your choice. But if you find out anything, come see me, and I'll tell you where you can go with it. No more pretending you're the cops, OK?"

"OK, Will, I'll see you soon." I put my hand out.

"Orville, the next time you come here, I won't be in bed. I promise. That's if you come here after nine."

He laughed and shook my hand firmly.

I rode my bike, smiling all the way home. I had a major sense of satisfaction. I had lifted Will's spirits and, for some reason, it didn't feel as though it was momentary. This might last, I thought. My negative side told me he might be in his bed on my next visit, but I wasn't going to listen to my negative side! I was too busy enjoying the idea of hope. Will also made the point that I had already accomplished a great deal so far as an investigator—something I hadn't even had time to think about, never mind to enjoy. I wanted to accomplish more. I wanted to find a killer, one who preyed upon a brittle old woman and a retired firefighter. I was pumped. My job had just begun!

Chapter
Eight

I CALLED MARK and told him we had to meet, and he told me he had to play miniature golf with Maria. Miniature golf and Maria took precedence over murder! I was definitely going to have to go solo the rest of the way.

I put on my Walkman, grabbed a pen and a notebook, and headed for the backyard. My parents had just bought a hammock, and I felt like breaking it in. I sank into the hammock and found instant comfort. The aroma from barbecue grills floated through the air, accompanied by a distant volleyballer's scream of "Out." I put in one of my mixed tapes and hummed away while jotting in my notebook "A list of suspects." I numbered it one to ten, and doodled to the sounds of The Pushstars, Better Than Ezra, The Dave Matthews Band, and the Bodeans. I don't remember feeling drowsy, but I must have still been tired from the night before, because I fell asleep. I dreamed about the fortune teller. She was shaking her head, saying "You don't remember everything." She said it over and over. I woke up, and for a second I didn't know where I was, because the yard was in complete darkness. The only light was provided by some fireflies having a party over by Mom's garden. What didn't I remember? I asked myself. I gathered up my list, which didn't have one name, and opened the screen door. What didn't I remember? I repeated as I walked into my house and realized I had fallen asleep on my headset and broken it. I was not too happy at seeing that, but there were more important things to be concerned about. I thought about what Will had said. I shouldn't take this dream for granted, I thought. What was it? And what was it about? Did I know who the killer was all this time? I had to think but I couldn't concentrate. The rest of my night was spent in tossing and turning and scattering bedsheets. I was getting frustrated but I had to keep faith in myself for Miss Sherwin's and Walter's sakes and who knows, the next possible victim.

A couple of days passed, and I didn't see myself solving the case. I really didn't have to blow off Mark when it came to the case; he had basically forgotten about it and was too busy blowing me off. He spent all his free time with Maria. We even stopped playing our daily Wiffle-ball game. I visited Will, who was out of bed and in a fine mood. He told me, "Rely on your senses. Cases aren't solved overnight. As long as you stay interested and keep aware, you'll have a shot." I listened to his words and went home and wrote them in my P.I. journal under the quotation, "You didn't remember everything!" For the next couple of days, I read both quotes before I went to bed.

It was getting on to mid-August, and hope was dwindling. I hadn't seen Walter or Martha Halloran, and I felt guilty. They probably figured I wasn't even trying. I would

visit Will, and he would give me advice on my attitude, but
he wouldn't direct me on how I should investigate. I was
becoming more and more negative. The back-to-school
commercials were on TV. The Red Sox were mathemati-
cally eliminated from the playoffs, and the Patriots were
in preseason. Mark and Maria were on their way to the
altar, and I had nothing to show for my summer of mystery except Miss Sherwin's confession, which I couldn't
show anyway. Life couldn't be any more depressing.

I sat down at the breakfast table and poured a glass
of orange juice. My mom was reading the *Belltown News*
to my father, who was trying not to burn the pancakes.

"What does the 'Around Town' column say?" Dad bel-
lowed over the sound of the kitchen fan.

My mother began reading. "I saw Bobby Norris, great
Little-League coach and all-around great guy. Geoff Myer,
Sr. still sells cars with a smile. Veronica Armstrong's
coffeecake sure hits the spot. Betsy Bishop, a selectwoman,
always selects class. Alfred and Nichole Sperry, fifty years
and still married. Bill Galley, sixty and sincere. Brian Honan,
new pool, can I take a dip? I saw Tom Anderson at Town
Hall; busy as a beaver, as usual, checking the zoning, with
a laugh. I saw Mary Timis and husband Al impersonate
Ginger Rogers and Fred Astaire at the Belltown Bank benefit. Mary Jacques, good luck in tutoring our future."

Mom stopped reading and said to Dad, "Hey! Isn't
that a great plug."

My parents were chatting about my mother's tutoring center, as I chomped on my cereal. Something stuck
out, but I couldn't place it. What was it?

"Mom, can you read that again?"

"Sure, Orville, I'd love to." She smiled and picked up the paper.

"Mary Jacques, good luck at tutoring our future."

"No, I'm sorry. A couple before that."

"Oh," she looked at me, confused.

"Umm, let's see. 'Brian Honan, new pool, can I take a dip? I saw Tom Anderson at the Town Hall, busy as a beaver, as usual checking the zoning, with a laugh. I saw Mary Timis . . .'"

"As usual, checking the zoning, with a laugh." I repeated.

"Yeah, Orville, What is it?"

"Nothing. I gotta get going," I said, suddenly in a hurry.

"What's the rush? I didn't think you worked today," my father asked.

"Well, I don't. I gotta meet a bunch of guys. We're going to play a pickup softball game," I lied. I had to get out of my house. My mind was working again. The floodgate had opened; and information and questions were flowing out at the same time. I thought I had remembered everything the fortune teller had told me. The words of advice I hadn't remembered were "Never overlook the obvious!" A simple observation, but somehow I had overlooked the obvious. Tom Anderson was a suspect in my mind. I had no proof, but I believed Will's advice: Trust your senses. Mr. Anderson was so interested in Miss Sherwin's house that he had asked Mary Timis when it would be "on the block" even before Miss Sherwin was cold in the grave. That could have been just a typical business move on his part, but maybe it was something more. I really didn't know, but for the first time, I had a suspect and it wasn't Walter!

The smell of tanning lotion lingered in the air as I pedaled past the beach. I ignored the laughing beach goers and kept my eyes focused on the road. Sweat was pouring off my brow, and the ocean was calling me for a quick dip, but I couldn't stop. I was about to break one of the most time-honored, sacred rules known to teenagers—I was going to the Belltown Library on a beach day! I closed my eyes and stood in the entrance for a few seconds. I opened my eyes and spotted two librarians staring at me with bulging eyes. Their stares were not mean; they looked amazed and confused. There is no doubt in my mind that I was the first kid to enter the library since June. The women kept whispering to each other until I approached the desk.

"Yes, may we help you, young man?" one of the librarians was able to muster.

"I'm, yes . . . I was wondering where you keep the back issues of the Belltown News?" I smiled, trying to break the tension in the room. They made me feel as though I were trying to buy beer with a fake ID. "Now, why would you want to look at the Belltown News?" the woman interrogated me.

"Why? What do you mean, why?" the question took me off guard.

She had a point, though. Why would anybody in his right mind want to look at back issues of the Belltown News on a sunny summer's day, or any day, for that matter.

A lot of the locals called it the Belltown Belch because it was usually so boring and short, without substance, except for the holidays. That's when it was boring and long!

"We have to know because we don't like letting people read the issues unattended—they might cut out articles or they might vandalize or draw bad pictures. So what is your purpose, young man?" She threw the question back at me.

"My purpose?" I was stalling. I didn't know what to say. I couldn't say, "Well, I think Mr. Anderson is a murderer and I want to look for some proof."

"Yes, your purpose. It isn't to deface town property, is it?" She was getting testy and her partner was actually reaching for the phone, if you can believe that.

"No, ma'am. The reason I want to see the back issues is that, you see, I want to write for the school newspaper this year. I thought if I spent a couple of hours reading how real number-one journalists write, I might get a few ideas for my own style and how can I improve it."

They both loved my sincerity; I must say that I did, too.

"Oh! It's so good to hear you respect the journalists who write for the Belltown News. My daughter, Olive Charles, writes 'The Arts and Crafts' column. You must be familiar with that?" She was beaming from ear to ear.

"Oh, yes, I am." I was trying to remember something about the column—how to make sweaters for cats?

"What can I say? That journalist knows her arts and crafts!"

"That's so kind of you. I'm always telling her she's a journalist, but she just laughs."

We kept talking about Olive Charles' Christmas bird feeders, Rice Krispie treats, pottery trays, and Popsicle-stick mailboxes. The mailboxes made me think of Joe Clancy— he could have his own post office by now. I finally passed the test and was allowed to go to the bottom floor and read through as many back issues of the Belltown News as I needed. I didn't exactly know what I was doing, but what else was new. I thought I was going to stumble onto something that would make my recent suspicions about Mr. Anderson correct.

I read for an hour, switching from papers from way back to papers that were just a couple of weeks old. I wasn't finding out anything except that I was right about Olive Charles. She must've had a thousand articles about how to make junk out of junk. I finally stopped reading. I had to think. I had to get a system.

Then I hypothesized. If Anderson killed Miss Sherwin and Mr. Saires for their land because it was zoned for business, what would have stopped him from doing it before? He owned half of Belltown.

After coming up with that theory, I decided to read just two parts of the newspaper, the obituary and the real estate section. I read the obituaries to find types like Miss Sherwin and Mr. Saires—old people who had no living relatives anybody knew about. I concentrated my search on the last ten years. It was depressing, spending all that time reading how different people had died. The ages ranged from kids younger than me to a guy a hundred and six. I tried to stay focused on the type of people I was looking for, but at times I would drift when reading about someone's life. I stopped drifting once my list began to lengthen. It took me three hours to find thirteen names that resembled the victims. I wrote down their names, the dates they died, the last known addresses, and the cause of death.

Name	Date Died	Address	Cause Of Death
1. Harold Tesson	September 16	39 Nickerson Rd.,	N.C. (Natural Causes)
2. Marion Princi	November 27	16 Cliff Rd.	N.C.
3. Carol Souza	December 17	102 Priscilla Ave.	N.C.
4. Mary Woods	February 12	58 Harbor Drive	N.C.
5. Diana Tate	April 6	28 Ocean Ave.	Accidental fall
6 Daniel Chase	May 4	32 Ocean Ave.	N.C
7. Emily Taskey	November 8	86 Ships Way	Car accident
8. Horace Nelson	January 22	4 Bell Buoy Rd.	Heart Attack
9. Maureen Quill	March 8	88 Ships Way	N.C
10. Samuel Rayner	May 28	12 Hillside Dr	Heart Attack
11. Joan Safflon	October 2	16 Hillside Dr.	N.C
12. Louise Sherwin	July 5	30 Beach View Rd.	Accidental fall
13. Brain Saires	July 17	38 Beach View Rd.	N.C

I didn't have to check the addresses. I knew those addresses from delivering the papers. The first four names and streets didn't match Anderson's buying schemes. It was the last nine that made me get that nervous feeling in the pit of my stomach. I was onto him. I looked through the real estate section, just to double-check. I didn't have to, but I had to be certain beyond a reasonable doubt.

I wrote down what I had found in the obituary notices and then in the listings in the real estate section.

On April 6, Diana Tate died of an accidental fall down her front stairs.

On May 1, Tom Anderson bought Diana Tate's house on Ocean Ave.

On May 4, Daniel Chase died in his house, of natural causes.

On June 12, Tom Anderson bought Daniel Chase's house. Daniel Chase's house was next to Diana Tate's house.

On July 12, the planning board approved Tom Anderson's proposal to knock down the two houses that were on land that was zoned for business, to build the Ocean View Fish Market.

Emily Taskey died November 8, when the brakes in her car failed and she drove off the road and hit a tree.

On February 25, Tom Anderson bought Emily Taskey's house.

On January 22 of the next year, Horace Nelson died of a heart attack from shoveling snow.

On April 17, Tom Anderson bought Mr. Nelson's house on Bell Buoy Road, which is on the corner of Ship's Way.

On March 8, Maureen Quill died of natural causes.

On July 2, Tom Anderson bought Maureen Quill's house.

The house was between Emily Taskey's and Horace Nelson's.

On September 12, Tom Anderson won approval of the planning board and the zoning board to knock down the three houses and build The Ship's Way Motel. The land was zoned for business, not for motels, but the zoning board approved Anderson's plan anyway, because, as one board member put it, "Anderson's businesses liven up Belltown." What a sick, ironic statement, I thought. I wrote like mad in my notebook.

On May 28, Samuel Rayner died of an apparent heart attack.

On September 1, Tom Anderson bought Mr. Rayner's house.

On October 2, Joan Saffron died in her home of natural causes.

On February 7, Tom Anderson bought Joan Saffron's house.

On January 30 of the next year, the planning board voted to let Tom Anderson go through with his proposal to build condominiums on the Hillside Drive property.

The last two names were Louise Sherwin and Brian Saires. I realized then that Miss Sherwin had screwed up Mr. Anderson's plans, whatever they were, by leaving the house to my family. Could owning Miss Sherwin's house put my family in danger? I wasn't sure. I knew I had nothing on Anderson—just a gut feeling. My gut told me he killed for land, but if I brought that to the authorities, they would just laugh and say, "He's just a businessman who happens to be at the right place at someone else's wrong time." The only question that stuck with me for a few minutes was, why didn't he just buy the houses, instead of killing the owners, and then buying the houses? After a few minutes spent looking at the victims' backgrounds, I was able to answer that question. All the victims were seventy-five or older. They all lived alone. They were all considered to be independent, some even reclusive. Their desire was probably to live their last days in their own homes. Any money offered probably wouldn't change their minds. They probably had no one they wanted to leave their money to. So why move from their homes? Of course, I could be all wrong. Maybe Anderson hadn't killed any of these people—perhaps he just saw his chance to cash in on their unfortunate deaths and took it. But I had that "gut thing" going, and I remembered what Will had told me. Listen to your senses. I was listening loud and clear, and my senses told me Tom Anderson was my killer!

It was early evening when I finally finished gathering all my information. I hung out on my front porch and went over all my notes, shaking my head. I had a major problem. If my theory was right about Anderson being the killer, who was going to believe me? Everybody respected the guy for his business savvy; he had never struck me as a bad guy, let alone a killer! I knew I had to see Will the next day and talk it over with him. I stopped reading my notes when I saw Joe Clancy across the street with a candle in his hand. He kept tilting the candle so the wax would drip onto the ground. Everything Joe did was strange. I watched him for about five minutes until my curiosity couldn't take it anymore. I got out from my lawn chair and went across his driveway.

"Hey, Joe, what's up?" I said while watching him take out a butter knife and scrape the wax off his driveway.

"Nothin' much, Jedi. Just experimenting on a way to help my fellow Jedis." He kept watching the ground.

"What do you mean?"

"I mean, look at that." He pointed to a G.I. Joe action figure on the driveway.

"Yeah. What about it?"

"Watch!" Joe then tilted the candle until the hot liquid covered the figure and quickly hardened.

"You see, Jedi, if we can learn how to carbonize action figures, we can learn how to carbonize the empire. And even better than that, by studying the carbonization process we can find a way to decarbonize Han Solo. We have to help Han Solo before it's too late."

Joe didn't even bat a lash. He was quite serious about his theory.

"Well, may 'The Force' be with you." I was not going to rain on his imagination. After all, who was I to tell him he was crazy? I was the one who thought the town's biggest developer was a murderer. I listened to Joe for a couple of minutes about how he intended to marry Princess Leia.

I walked away from Joe laughing at myself. I was going over my prime suspect, and I was distracted by a kid waxing action figures. I was about to open my door when the voice froze my body.

"Orville!"

I turned around to see Maria standing in my front yard.

"Oh, hi, Maria!" I walked towards her. My legs were wobbling; I felt like Bambi taking his first steps. I probably looked just as clumsy.

"What's up?" I tried to say casually. Her scent danced in the August breeze. She looked amazing.

"I have to talk to you, Orville. Can we go on your porch in the backyard?"

I was shivering and it wasn't from the breeze.

"Yeah, we can go to the backyard."

"Good, 'cause I think we should be alone."

I couldn't believe it. I was finally going to be alone with the girl of my dreams. I had to stay in control and not say something stupid. When we got to the backyard, Maria sat on the edge of the hammock and I sat in a lawn chair in front of her.

"Orville, I had to come see you. I didn't know who else to tell, and I figured I could talk to you." The tone in Maria's voice sounded worried.

"You can talk to me. What's wrong?"

"Well, you know how I work at Mr. Anderson's motel." She stopped.

"Yeah, what about it?" Anderson's name made me hurry my response.

"Well, you see, I was working yesterday afternoon, and I heard him talking on the phone. He was yelling loudly at his lawyer or someone."

"What'd he say?"

"He said your parents screwed up all of his plans. He kept talking about how angry he was that your mom wouldn't sell Miss Sherwin's house." Maria paused for my reaction.

I just nodded for her to continue.

"He kept screaming into the phone, telling his lawyer, or whoever it was, that they had to go with the other plan. He said if Mrs. Lyons doesn't accept the offer on her house that, that he'd, he'd ah . . ."

"He'd what?" I digged.

"He'd make her 'take a bath like Louise.' Orville, I think he was talking about Louise Sherwin. I know he was, 'cause it wasn't like he was angry. It was like he was crazy or something. I don't know what to do."

Maria was scared, and it angered me to see that Anderson had this effect on her. I was wrestling with what I knew and what she had told me. I wasn't sure if I should tell her what I knew. The way she was shaking while telling me, I figured I should keep my information to myself. Why frighten her more? I had to do something because I knew Mrs. Lyons fit the description of the other victims. She was old, she lived alone, and she used to run a beauty parlor out of her basement, so the house had to be zoned for business. And, again, I thought, she lives just two doors up from the Sherwin house.

I knew what I had to do.

"Maria, Mr. Anderson was probably just angry. You should forget about it. But when do you work the front desk again?"

"I work it tonight, in about an hour. Why?" She was puzzled.

"Well, isn't Anderson's office near the front desk?"

"Yeah, why?"

I could see she was trying to put it all together. "Well, because he's not around at night, right?" "Right," she nodded.

"Well, I'll come by and take a peek in his office, just to be sure."

"Oh, I don't know, Orville. I don't know if it's safe, and, anyway, what if you got caught? That could go on your record."

"You make it sound like I already have one. Don't worry about me. But Maria, one question."

"What's that, Orville?"

Even when she was scared she looked beautiful.

"Why'd you tell me and not Mark or somebody else?"

"Well 'cause I was worried about your parents and also the fact that you caught two robbers, and I thought you might have some ideas."

"Oh, OK. Well, I'll see you at ten o'clock."

"OK, Orville. Be careful. I'll leave the master key in the plant on the table, right in front of his office."

"OK. See you later, Maria."

I knew I was dealing with a killer, and I had to get more proof, not just for Maria's sake—and mine—but for Mrs. Lyons. She would be the next victim if I didn't act fast.

Chapter Nine

THE HANDS ON my kitchen clock inched along like a slug on a Sunday stroll. I fidgeted at the kitchen table, killing time by going over my list for THE PROPER EQUIPMENT FOR A BREAK-IN:

(1) Flashlight—check. (2) Spy camera—semi-check. All I had was a disc camera; that would have to do. (3) Black clothes—semi-check. I had navy-blue shorts and the only black shirt I had was a U2 concert T-shirt with a black-and-white picture of Bono and the guys on the front. (4) Gloves—another semi-check. The only gloves I could find were my batting gloves, and they were kind of worn. (5) Pocket-sized recorder—check. I figured I'd bring my dad's tape recorder, so if I found any evidence that I couldn't take a picture of, or if the picture didn't come out, I'd still be able to describe everything in detail without leaving any parts out. I got the idea from a "Magnum, P.I." rerun, or was it "Mystery!" on PBS? Anyway, whatever it was, the guy had tape recorded himself reading documents but, later in the show, he got amnesia from a car accident, and he was still able to solve the case because he had the in-

formation on tape. I think it was "Mystery!" I don't really remember.

Well, back to my list. I knew I had all the equipment I needed, and Maria was going to leave the key in the plant, so I was pretty well prepared except for one thing—I was scared! It was not as if I broke into places all the time. What if I got caught? I would get into major trouble with the cops and my parents. My parents let a lot slide, but breaking and entering is where they'd put their four feet down, probably down my throat! The worst-case scenario was if Anderson himself caught me! I knew I had to stop thinking about it and just do it, like calling a girl for the first time. The more you think about it, the worse it gets, but once you begin talking, things are all right, usually. That's why I guess I was kind of relieved when the hands on my clock finished their journey at 9:55. I stuffed the gloves into my back pocket, the pocket-sized tape recorder into my right pocket, and hung the disc camera around my neck, and under my shirt.

When I got to the motel, I stood outside for a minute. My senses were alive. I could taste summer trying to hang on. It was a warm night, but a breeze would come along now and then. Not a July breeze, where the air is blowing, but a breeze that told me it wouldn't be long until sweaters and backpacks. The crickets seemed to know summer was almost over; they were having their last hurrah. I looked up to the sky and said, "If you're home, God, I really need your help tonight!"

The stars distracted me. They made the sky look like one huge LiteBrite machine. I laughed at how corny my analogy was, and I knew that Sandra Vincent would appreciate it, being the queen of game boards. I stopped laughing and thought, where did those days go of being a little kid playing with the LiteBrite machine! It was so simple back then; now, here I was, still young and alive but in the middle of life and death. I prayed to God one more time, took a deep breath, and opened the door quickly.

Once I got into the lobby, my body began moving itself. I walked briskly past the front desk and gazed over in Maria's direction. She was talking to an elderly couple, suggesting a good place for breakfast for the next day. She saw me but kept her eye contact on the couple so they wouldn't turn around and see me. I walked about forty feet down a hall and came to Anderson's office. The plant was on a table right outside his office. The plant was the type with all the leaves hanging out over the pot, so I couldn't see the key. I had to feel for it. I scanned the pot with my hand, and I wasn't making any progress. It was taking too long. This was supposed to be the easy part, and all I kept doing was grabbing handfuls of dirt. Sweat began forming on my brow and dripped onto my glasses. I was getting dirty and a little disoriented. Finally, I got on my knees and dug my head between the hanging leaves and looked for the key. I saw the key taped to the side of the flowerpot. I thought Maria had said she'd leave the key in the pot, not outside. I ripped the key off the pot and began to get up. I stopped and almost knocked the plant over when I heard a loud bang in back of me. Someone is behind me, I thought. I couldn't move. I was thinking of getting up and running when I heard the bang again. I slowly turned around to face the enemy—the ice machine down the hall, spitting out ice cubes every couple of minutes. I was relieved for half a second until I saw a guy and girl approaching me.They looked like college kids.

"Hey, man, what are you doing?" the guy said, pointing at me on my hands and knees in front of the plant. I didn't know what to say, so I gave the great ad lib.

"Nothin', man."

The girl started laughing.

"Larry, I know what he's doing," she turned to the guy.

"What? What is he doing?" he began laughing, too.

"He's gardening." She pointed at me and then the plant. "That doesn't look right at this time of night. I'm going to the desk."

"No, don't," I said. "I just found my key. I had dropped it."

I finally got up from the floor and gave them a wave as they went to the front desk. I could hear them asking Maria questions, and I knew from the way she was stalling that she must've heard them with me. I put the key in the lock and opened the door without a problem. I was psyched to see that there were no windows in Anderson's office so I didn't have to use the flashlight. I turned the switch and the lights came on instantly. I was expecting a real fancy office, considering that Anderson owned half the town. It was anything but fancy.

It had the normal office stuff: a desk, a lounge chair, a couple of file cabinets, and a bluefish hanging on the wall.

I went over to the file cabinets and tried opening them. They were locked. I was kicking myself that I could be so naive to think I could just open the file cabinets, and a signed, sealed confession would be there, waiting for me. I decided to check Anderson's desk for something that I could use to jiggle the lock. He kept his desk very neat, and he had nothing personal in it. It just had paper and pens, empty folders—that kind of stuff. I pulled a letter opener out and decided to try it. I had seen a rerun of "Remington Steele" and he was using one, but I wasn't "Remington Steele." The lock wouldn't budge, so I went to put the letter opener back when it hit me: I had forgotten to put on my gloves. I was getting scared at my stupidity and pulled out the gloves from my back pocket. I dropped one on the floor, and as I reached down to grab it, I spotted two switches on the side of the desk. I flipped the first switch, and I couldn't believe what I switched on. The paneled wall with the bluefish opened up.

It was like something out of a James Bond movie. Right before my eyes there was a small hidden room. I took out my tape recorder and began whispering in it, "I just uncovered a hidden room in Tom Anderson's office. I am going to go into it. There is a model on the table. The model is of an amusement park. Oh, my god!" The model was an amusement park on land right next to the motel. It read "Anderson's Amusements By The Sea." I kept talking into the tape recorder, giving every detail about the amusement park. The model was designed to the tee. It had a Ferris wheel, roller coaster, game rooms, even water fountains. The restrooms were going to be built on Louise

Sherwin's land! I took out my camera and began snap-
ping shots. Anderson was planning on buying or taking
six other houses in my area. He was going to build an
amusement park right next to his motel! What a tourist
trap! I didn't understand how Anderson could have a
project like that passed by a town that sells Mother Na-
ture to the tourists, but he probably had a plan. There was
also a file cabinet in the secret room. It wasn't locked. He
probably figured, why lock it if nobody knows about it
anyway? In the cabinet were files that detailed his plans
to buy Louise Sherwin's land—plans that had been thrown
a curve by Miss Sherwin's bequest to my parents. Anderson had scribbled the following notes: "House given to
Jacques family. Won't sell! Comment: Will sell! Who would
want to own a house by an amusement park? Nobody!
Who would want their child to be tutored next to an
amusement park? Nobody! WILL SELL!"

My heart was jumping, and I was drenched with sweat.
I knew I was positively right about the guy! It wasn't just
my crazy imagination. Tom Anderson was a killer. I skimmed
through the other files about the motel. They seemed
meaningless. Then I came across a file on Mr. Saires. It read
"Won't sell! Will have to buy, anyway!" I took out my camera and tried to take a picture, but I was out of film. Extra
film hadn't been on my checklist! I was beginning to get
excited about the information I had found, but I was also
becoming more and more paranoid. I shut the cabinet
quickly and slipped into the other room. I turned the
switch off, and the wall closed in, and everything was back
to normal. I eyed the other switch for a couple of seconds,

debating whether I should flip it. My curiosity was too much, and I flipped the switch on. Nothing happened. At least, I thought nothing happened! I waited a few seconds, and then it struck me what that switch was for—a silent alarm!

My body was moving quicker than my mind, and the result was I was fumbling and stumbling, trying to get out of the room. I heard a knock on the door. My first instinct, and a bad one at that, was to hide in the closet. As I jumped into the completely pitch-black closet, I bumped into some coats, and something crashed onto the ground. My brains finally took hold: hiding in the closet was probably the most ridiculous thing I could have done. I opened the closet door, and the knocking continued, but now it was followed by a voice, "Orville, get out of there, quick!" It was Maria, and she didn't have to say it twice. I opened the door and she pointed toward another room. "Go in the laundry room, go out the back window. I'll stall them. Quick! Go!" she urged. I handed her the key and then followed her instructions. I jumped right out the window, just missing the back of a parked cop car with no lights.

Sergeant Gonestone didn't see me jump out of the window, but he did see me try to sneak by his car. "Hey, Jacques! Stop right there!" he screamed.

I froze. I was busted.

"We don't need you here to play cops and robbers again. So get outta here, or I'll charge you with disrupting an investigation!" He pointed for me to leave. I just nodded. I knew if I said anything it would delay my getaway. My heart was going to burst through my U2 shirt. I managed a quick look into the motel's lobby and saw Maria talking with the police and an irate Tom Anderson. What was she telling them, I wondered. I knew she would tell me soon. The question was what could I tell her.

I raced back to my backyard and waited for Maria. I knew, with all the confusion it would probably be a long wait, but I needed the time to cool down and think. My mind was racing in a million directions, and I absolutely knew that Tom Anderson was a killer, and I had to do something quick. I thought about telling my dad, but all he could do was notify the police, and I wasn't sure that all the cops were clean! I mean, Maria heard Anderson talking to someone, so he could have had somebody working for him, maybe more than one! I had to go to Will. He would know exactly what to do. It eased my mind that I at least had Will to help me. I had the craziest feeling: I was scared about Anderson, but I was also excited about seeing Maria. If I'm thinking about this girl during a murder case, I must really like her, I thought. At that moment, I looked up and Maria was right in front of me. I felt stupid because I jumped a little. But she gave me an understanding look. We were both rattled. We began talking at the same time until I stopped and let her continue.

"Did you find anything?" she asked, out of breath.

"Well," I still didn't know what to say.

"C'mon Orville. Did you find anything out?" she demanded.

"Well, you see, Maria, I, ah, ah, I think that there might be some truth to what you heard." I said it!

"You mean he's a killer!" she yelled.

"Keep your voice down, will you? . . . . All I know is whatever I tell you, you have to keep to yourself. I'm not joking around here. This is not kid's stuff, you hear me?"

She nodded. Then I rethought what I had said, and I was still a little reluctant to tell her. "Maybe it's better you don't know," I said, out of desperation, but I knew she knew too much to shut her mind off.

"No, c'mon, tell me."

I decided not to fight the inevitable, and I told Maria everything I had done and found out. At times, throughout my story, she choked, "Oh, my god!"

"Now, do you think you can trust this Will?" she asked.

"What?"

"Can he really help you? I mean, he's in a mental hospital."

"I can trust Will with my life, and I figure he must have some connections, like someone I can contact for help."

"OK. Well, you know him better than I do," she admitted.

I was beginning to feel comfortable with Maria. The awkwardness was turning into confidence. I mean, I'm not bragging, but my adventure gave me some merit in her eyes, or at least so I thought.

"So, now it's my turn for questioning," I said.

She nodded "Yes."

"What did you tell Anderson and Gonestone?"

"I told the cops that I heard someone breaking into Mr. Anderson's office and pulled the alarm."

"Did they buy it?"

"Gonestone did, but Anderson grilled me with all sorts of questions—but I just pretended I was scared and he let up."

"I was really worried about you, Orville," she said, as she reached over and gave me a hug. I closed my eyes and savored every second of her embrace. It seemed like all of my sleepless nights were in that hug. We finally pulled back and our eyes froze again. I slowly inched my face towards her. I wasn't nervous. It just seemed so right. I kissed her softly. Nothing mattered in the world except this moment. I was kissing the girl of my dreams, and the reality was better. After about thirty seconds Maria jerked her head and moved away from me.

"Orville, what do you think you're doing?"

The blood was flowing to my face. It must've been a crimson red.

"What?" I managed.

"What! Why are you kissing me? You know I go out with Mark who happens to be your best friend!"

I felt like I'd been shot. I know that's a weak analogy, but that's how I felt. Part of me was in complete disbelief that I had misread her actions, and another part of me felt dizzy and in pain. She stood there with arms crossed, waiting for an answer.

"I thought … y'know … you … ah … hugged me … and …"

"I hugged you because I was worried about you, not because I liked you, see." She was more toned down and in control.

I had to get away quick because my emotions had

gone from one extreme to the other, and I knew I was going to get sick—the bad sick! I don't think there will ever be a more embarrassing moment in my life. I had to get away!

"I see. I better get going. I'll talk to you later."

"You don't have to leave," she said.

I wanted to shake her and say, "Can't you tell how I feel? Don't give me 'I don't have to leave.'" I had to leave, all right. I might as well move out of town!

"I have to go to work tomorrow."

I think I felt safer hiding in Anderson's closet.

"OK. We'll keep in touch after you talk to Will."

She acted like the whole event was over. I'd keep in touch . . . YEAH, RIGHT! I nodded, and dashed into my house.

When I finally gained my composure, which took forever, I decided to go over my notes and update them. I had to do something to take my mind off Maria. I figured there couldn't be any more emotion I could feel—I was drained. Then I got a large lump in my throat when I reached into my pocket for the tape recorder, and it wasn't there. I looked around the room. Maybe I took it out and, without thinking, I put it somewhere in my room, I hoped. I was frantic, running upstairs, downstairs. It went on and on, and then I knew—the bang in Anderson's closet! I must've dropped the tape recorder in Anderson's closet. I dragged my body into the bathroom and threw up. My stomach couldn't take it any more, and I couldn't either! I passed out on the bathroom floor.

Chapter
Ten

WHEN I CAME to, I picked up my stiff body off the cold tiles. The rush of fear from the night before was back in full force. I threw some cold water on my face while trying to figure out a plan. The first thing I had to do was call Boom Boom and see if he could work for me. Then I had to see Will. I just hoped to God that Anderson wouldn't find my tape recorder before I could get help!

I called Boom Boom; he leaped at the chance of working for me. The man loved to work. I got off the phone and began to move fast, because if my parents saw me not going to work, they would want to know why and I didn't have time to think up a good excuse. I ripped off my U2 shirt, which smelled bad from the nerves of the night before. I opened my closet of twenty-plus concert T-shirts and grabbed the first one on the rack. It was a white "Bim Skala Bim" number, from a Boston ska band that was huge with me and my friends. I changed and then grabbed all my notes. I sneaked down the stairs and was heading out the back door when I heard my father talking to someone on the front porch. My dad didn't sound his usual laid-back self. He sounded annoyed. I stopped my escape and listened.

"Look, I don't know how many times I've got to tell you, Tom, it's not about money. We just don't want to sell."

The other voice was insistent. "I'm offering you a lot of money. I mean, a lot of money. You have to at least sit down with your wife and consider the offer. Consider your children. How are you going to afford college in a few years? You're just a schoolteacher."

"First of all, I don't much care for the way you use the word 'just'—that offends me."

"What I mean . . ."

"No, I know what you mean! You think you can buy and sell your way around this town without any regard to other people. Money isn't everything. You see, Tom, my wife left teaching to rear our children. She now has the opportunity to go back to doing something she loves, and no amount of money is going to change our minds."

"I can get her a tutoring job at Lillian White's center."

"You just don't get it, do you! This is her dream, and she's going to do it. So thank you for your offer, but NO!"

I peeked through the screen door to see Anderson's reaction. He was shaking his head in disgust. My dad stood in front of him, with his arms folded. I turned to go to the back door, and as I turned I heard my dad call my name. I turned my head slightly and saw my dad beckoning me with his hand to come outside. "God, don't speak," I said to myself. I knew if Anderson heard the sound of my voice, and then found the tape recorder, I was dead!

"Mr. Anderson, this is my son, Orville. Do you know Orville?"

The anger on Anderson's face began to fade. I could tell he was putting on a fake smile for my sake, and I knew why my dad had me come outside to change the subject and then get rid of Anderson.

"I don't know Orville, but I've heard a lot about him and how he helped catch those robbers earlier this summer. Good to meet you," he put out his hand.

Talk about shaking hands with the devil! I took a firm grip and just nodded. My dad turned his attention to me, "Why aren't you at work?"

They both stared at me. Anderson was looking me up and down; maybe if I didn't know the truth, I would have thought nothing of it, but I did know the truth! My dad waited for an answer as I looked down to the ground. I was shaking again. I finally looked up and pointed to my throat.

"Sore throat?" Anderson guessed.

I nodded, and Anderson and I made eye contact. It was like I could see beyond the business discussion. If I didn't know, I probably wouldn't have seen anything in his eyes. But I did know, and his eyes seemed naked. They told me what he really was. Maybe that doesn't make a lot of sense, but it made a lot when our eyes met. Apparently, I was not the only one who felt that way. Anderson seemed a little uneasy himself as he looked down to the ground.

"Well, gee, your throat must be sore if you're not talking," said my dad turning to Anderson. "Usually, we can't shut Orville up."

He laughed and Anderson nodded, simulating a laugh but not actually making any noise. He was staring at me again.

"Well, you better rest up, Orville," Dad suggested.

I kept nodding. I turned and began walking away from them, toward the door.

"Orville," Anderson's voice caught me before I made it to the door. I turned and our eyes began wrestling again.

"It was nice meeting you," he said confidently. I gave him one last nod before I escaped into the safety of my house.

My sore-throat excuse helped me when it came to not talking to Anderson, but it imprisoned me in my bed for a couple of hours. My parents finally left for the beach around noon. I jumped out of my bed, grabbed my notes, got on my bike, and headed to see Will. I knew this was it. I had the information, and now it was time to do something with it. There was no one at the front desk of the hospital, so I decided to go to Will's room. I was a little nervous as I began to open his door. I prayed that he wouldn't be depressed. I opened the door and looked around the room—no Will. The bed was made, the curtains were wide open, and the sun was spilling onto the floor. There were even tulips in a vase on the counter. The room didn't look depressing at all—it looked alive and happy. It didn't look like Will's room at all. A man popped his head into the room. I could tell he was a guest by the clothes he wore, and he seemed a little different.

"What you lookin' for?" He licked his lips with his tongue.

"Oh, hi! I'm looking for Will."

"Will? Who's that?" he looked confused.

"The guy who lives in this room."

"Oh, you mean Bill?"

"Well, maybe Bill." Maybe some of the guests called him Bill, I thought.

"He's dead," the man said nonchalantly.

"He's DEAD?" I was stunned, shaken. "What do mean, he's dead? I just saw him the other day!"

"What a difference a day makes," he stated. "He had a heart attack last night. He's dead."

My feelings were all tangled up. I wanted to cry. I wanted to scream. I wanted to hide, but most of all, I didn't want to believe. I couldn't believe this man, and I kept grilling him with questions. I must've been pretty loud, because Mrs. Harris opened the door and wasn't her usual pleasant self.

"What the heck is going on here?" she demanded.

"Will's dead!"

"What? What are you talking about, Orville?" her eyes popped out.

"This guy says Will is dead!" I pointed to the guest. Mrs. Harris turned and yelled into the hall, "Dennis!" Two seconds later, a worker appeared at the doorway and waited for Mrs. Harris's instructions.

"Dennis, can you help Mr. Foley back to his room?"

Mrs. Harris then turned to me and smiled. "Will's not dead."

"But that guy?" I pointed toward the hallway.

"Yes, you'll have to forgive Mr. Foley. He gets a little

confused now and then. You see, one of our guests did pass on last night, but it was in the next room. Mr. Foley just got a little confused."

She smiled. She could see my relief, and I cracked a smile.

"Well, where is Will?"

"Come over here." Mrs. Harris skipped towards the window and pointed, "Look down there, Orville."

I looked down and spotted Will tossing horseshoes.

"Will came to me the other day and asked if I could get him some horseshoes. He loved throwing them when he was a boy. I would never have dreamed that he'd be out there enjoying the day. I know why he is finally coming around."

She stopped looking out the window and looked at me. "Why?" I asked.

"Because he feels he has something to live for. Your friendship. I know people think I'm out in left field sometimes with my methods, but I observe a lot. Some of these guests need all sorts of chemical help, and others need just to know someone cares. That's Will. He had nobody, but then you came along, and he's alive again."

I was beaming and nodding.

"And, Orville, he is not the only person who's benefited. You have made a loyal friend."

I could hear the excitement in her voice, and I was also feeling good. Will was not just someone I was getting help from. He was indeed my friend.

"Oh, by the way, Orville."

"Yes, Mrs. Harris?"

"Just between you and me, I always knew who it was reading magazines in the waiting room," she winked.

My smile became even wider. Mrs. Harris knew more than Will gave her credit for, and that's how her method worked. She allowed Will to think he was tricking her because she hoped that he'd connect with a visitor. He did! Mrs. Harris was all right!

When I got outside and caught Will's attention, he put his horseshoes down and walked over to me, limping. I had never noticed the severe limp before, probably because I had never seen him walk before. He knew I had some information, so we skipped the greetings.

"Whatcha got, Orville?"

"Where do I start?" I said, looking down at my notebook.

"Let's go over to the picnic table," Will suggested.

I told him everything, and he gave the same response throughout my story—a simple nod. When I finally finished, he waited a few seconds and then smiled and said, "Orville, I think you've got your man. Now what I want you to do is go to the Belltown Police Station."

"I don't know, Will," I interrupted.

"Hear me out, Orville, I'm not finished," he said, matter-of-factly.

"I want you to go see this man." He gave me a slip of paper that read: "Detective Shane O'Connell."

"Shane O'Connell? I've never heard of him," I said.

"I know, he's new on the force. He just moved here, and thank God, he did," Will sighed.

"How do you know I can trust him, and how do you

know he'll even believe me?" I questioned.

"Believe me, Orville. You can trust this young man. But when you tell him, make sure you go for a drive and tell him. Don't tell him in the station 'cause you don't know if this Anderson guy owns dirty cops. I doubt he does. Maybe you better get going now. Hey, what time is it?"

"I don't know. I don't wear a watch."

"I know you don't. Why?" He reached into his pocket.

"I don't 'cause my wrists are thin. Watches look kinda stupid."

"Don't worry about your wrists. They'll get thicker. Here." He handed me a watch. As I put it on, I noticed an inscription on the back: "To Will, Love Katherine."

"Why are you giving me this?" I was confused and flattered at the same time.

"A detective should always know the time, and a good detective should know better than anyone," he smiled.

"I can't take this." I tried giving it back.

"Why? 'Cause of your wrists?"

"No, because someone gave it to you."

"Please keep it. I know Katherine would've been honored to have you wear it. Always be aware of the time," he said softly. He seemed to be thinking; then he broke out of it and said, "What are you doing sitting there? You've got a killer to catch!"

"I'll wear it with pride." I meant every word of it. Will laughed.

"Orville, don't get sappy now, you sound like Mrs. Harris."

As I rode my bike to the Belltown Police Station, I

thought of Mrs. Harris, and Will, and I felt a little more comfortable about my situation. It was indeed ironic that I was not only there for Will but that he was there for me. Mrs. Harris was right. Will was not the only person who had benefited from my visits!

I walked into the Belltown Police Station, and the first person to greet me was none other than Sergeant Gonestone.

"What do you want, Jacques?" he greeted me, with a scowl.

"Sergeant, I'd like to talk to Detective O'Connell," I smiled.

"Now, what do you want to talk to O'Connell about?"

He folded his arms. On the bike ride over, I had thought that I'd bump into Gonestone, so I was ready for his question. I figured the "journalist bit" worked great at the library—why not use it again?

"You see, Sergeant, school is just around the corner."

"And?" his eyebrows furrowed.

"And I'm going to write for the school paper, and I'd like to write an article about the new detective."

"Why would you write about O'Connell?" He was confused.

"Because this year, the school is offering a criminology class, and I thought that writing about the detective might spark interest in the students to find out what police work is all about."

"Why don't you write about a regular policeman, y'know, like me, instead of a detective?" Gonestone wouldn't quit on me, and now he was having visions of his name in ink. I paused for a second, but I was able to make a quick rebound.

"Well, I do plan on interviewing you, if it's OK, but I know I'd have to make an appointment first, because you're so busy, right?"

"Of course. In fact, right now I have to check on some serious business."

"OK, Sergeant, I'll be in touch."

Gonestone gave a serious squint and went out the door.

Detective O'Connell's office was down the hall past the Traffic Ticket Office. There was a receptionist outside his office. Pretty impressive, having a receptionist in this town, I thought.

"May I help you, young man?" she asked.

"Yes, I'd like to see Detective O'Connell."

"What's this in regard to?"

"I'd like to interview him for the school paper."

"OK, and what's your name?"

"Orville Jacques."

She picked up the telephone, spoke quietly, and then asked me to go into Detective O'Connell's office.

When I walked into Detective O'Connell's office, he was on the phone, and he put his hand up and motioned me to come in. He then put his index finger up as if to say,

"Wait one second." He was talking to someone about the growing drug problem and crime rate in Belltown. I half-listened but I began to look around his office. There were pictures, degrees, and all the normal stuff, but what really caught my eye was an autographed baseball in a holder on his desk. I wanted to pick it up and try to make out the names, but I knew that might not be polite. He must've been watching, because I heard him say, "Wait one second, Mel. Go ahead, check out the autographs."

I looked up, surprised, "Oh thanks." I picked up the ball and there were only two names signed on it but it was two of the best names ever—Pedro Martinez and Nomar Garciaparra! I stared at the beautiful, black cursive writing and got lost in Red Sox memories. I finally looked over at Detective O'Connell, and he gave me the thumbs-up while he finished up on the phone. I smiled and gave him a thumb way up. Then he hung up.

"Hi. Detective Shane O'Connell." He put his hand out.

"Hi. Orville Jacques." I shook his hand , smiling.

"Orville, that's a unique name."

"That's a nice way to put it," I laughed.

"So, Orville, you like Pedro and Nomar?"

"Who around here wouldn't?"

"Yankee fans."

I laughed, "Even they have to respect those guys. We're talking about the greatest pitcher the Sox ever had, and next to Ted Williams, the greatest hitter. Did you know Nomar played in the Cape Cod League for the Orleans Cardinals back when he was going to Georgia Tech?"

"Wow, you know your Sox. You might like to know

they're classy guys off the field as well. They do some work for an organization I used to volunteer for called Read Across America. They want kids to get into reading because it really can change your life. Do you like to read?"

"Yeah. Yeah." I wasn't listening to his question, "Oh, man, so you know them?"

He laughed, "Well enough to know that those autographs are real. I could tell you a story though about a guy I once busted for selling merchandise that had forged autographs. But we're not here for that. So you want to interview me for the newspaper?"

He leaned on the edge of the desk. It took me a second to get my train of thought back, but then I said, "Well, not exactly."

"My receptionist said ..."

"I have to talk to you about something private, and I can't let anybody else know or I could be in danger."

"Orville, let me get my coat, and we'll go for a little drive."

I was hoping he would say that, and a wave of relief went up my spine when he did. He got his coat and we talked about sports as we walked out of the station. I was feeling pretty confident that he would listen to me with an open mind, just by the respect he was showing me. Besides, he was a Red Sox fan, and that told me a lot. We got into his brown van, and he began driving down by the beach. Once we passed the Belltown Yacht Club he turned to me and said, "First of all, Orville, please call me Shane. I mean, I'm only thirty-two, and I'm still getting used to being called Detective. So, for now just call me Shane, all right?"

I nodded in agreement.

"OK. Now just tell what you've got to tell me, and I won't ask any questions until you're done."

I nodded again and thought that that must be a detective procedure or something because that's how Will went about business. I began telling my story and Shane just drove along nodding, as if nothing fazed him. Then I got to the part when I broke into Anderson's motel, and he spoke for the first time.

"Shut up, Orville!" He looked over at me.

"What?"

"Shut up. I don't want to know what you're going to tell me about last night because that would mean that I knew you were involved in a crime last night. I don't know that, do I?"

He pulled the van into the beach parking lot and turned the engine off.

I understood exactly. I couldn't implicate myself in the breakin at Anderson's motel. I had to choose my words carefully— "What I'm saying is, I have reason to believe that Anderson wants to build an amusement park on some of his motel land; some of the evidence could be in his office."

Shane gave a wink. He was relieved I had gotten his point. Being a cop, he would have had to arrest me, but he caught me just in time. I showed Shane all my notes, and he analyzed them, going over dates and names of victims. Finally, he said, "Well, this is incredible."

"You don't believe me?"

"No. What's incredible is that I do. I'm shocked that none of the cops saw this pattern."

"Welcome to Belltown."

"Yeah, I'm beginning to see that. Now, you can't tell anybody about this. Just let me go to work on it. I'll begin surveillance on Anderson after I drop you off."

"There's something I didn't tell you." I couldn't tell him Maria and Will knew, but I had to somehow let him know that I'd left the tape recorder in Anderson's closet.

"What haven't you told me, Orville? I don't like the sound of this."

"Remember the stuff I shouldn't talk about?"

"Yes. Go on, carefully."

"Well, there was this tape recorder left in that certain place with a voice on tape that could resemble someone you're talking to." I cringed and waited for his response.

"What? Oh, my God! A case like this takes time to build. If he finds the tape recorder, he could be out of town tonight. Does he know your voice?" Shane snapped.

"I don't think so," I answered.

"Well, 'I don't think so' is not good enough for me. Where did you drop it?" He wasn't tiptoeing about what he should know anymore.

"In the closet."

"Are you sure?"

"I'm positive."

"Well, that's not too bad. We just have to hope that what you heard him say about Mrs. Lyons was true. If it is true, he'll probably strike soon. But if he finds that tape recorder, then we'll just have to go with what you have so far, but all that evidence can be admissible. It would build a stronger case if we caught this guy in the act. I shouldn't say this, but I will. Do you want to help stake him out?"

I couldn't believe it. I was psyched, and there was no way I could hide it.

"YES!"

"Now, I'm only letting you come along because I would feel safer knowing you're with me in case he does find the tape recorder and puts it all together. Also, as unprofessional as it may be to let you come—God knows I could get in some very hot water—I think you deserve to ride this thing out. You've done great work!"

"Wow, thanks! What am I going to tell my parents about staying out late tonight?"

"Give them that journalist spiel, get something to eat, and I'll pick you up in an hour."

He started the engine and drove me to my doorstep. My parents were a little upset that I had missed work because of the alleged sore throat; they weren't thrilled that now I wanted to go out and watch a detective drive around. My mom was especially upset because she wanted to know what would happen if the detective was called to the scene of a crime or something. I said, "Crime in this town?" and laughed. They both laughed. If only they had known . . .

The crickets' songs became shorter and shorter as the days went by. I guess I had seen too many cop shows. I was expecting Anderson to make a move the first night. Reality proved that being a detective was not always exciting. In fact, sitting in Shane's van, watching Anderson's house, was downright boring. The only good part about it was talking sports with Shane. He knew his sports.

On the fourth night, my parents told me it was the last night I could drive around town with Shane. As my dad put it, "You're writing for the school paper, not The *Washington Post!*" Shane picked me up and we went to the drive-in of Bill's Donuts. We both got large coffees. He got two sugars, and I got four. We parked about four houses up from Anderson's house. When we got settled I took the lid off my coffee and threw it on the dash. Shane reached over and took the lid off the dash and gave it back to me.

"Orville, number one rule for being a detective: Never throw a coffee lid on the dash of the car you're using during a stakeout."

"Why's that?" I was confused.

"Once there was this detective who was the best at surveillance. I mean, nobody could smell him. But one day, out of the blue, a guy he was watching casually walked up to the detective's car, pulled out a gun, and blew him away."

"If the guy was so good watching, how'd he get caught?"

"That's what everyone wanted to know. So when they caught the guy who killed the detective, they asked him. Do you know what he told them?"

"No. What?"

"He said he walked by the car and saw coffee lids and faded circles on the dash, and he thought to himself that only cops have time to drink that much coffee in their cars."

Shane turned his attention to his coffee and took a sip.

"Wow!" I took the lid and put it in the Bill's Donuts bag.

We spent the next twenty minutes talking about the Patriots' chances of making the playoffs and Boston College's chances of making it to a major bowl game. Shane then asked me if I had a girlfriend. I figured, since he was kind of like my partner, I could tell him about Maria and what had happened. As I was telling him, I thought to myself that I better meet with Maria and tell her I have someone on the case! When I finished telling him how she totally made me feel like a fool, he began laughing.

"What's so funny?" I wasn't amused.

"Sorry, Orville, it just reminds me of the first girl I liked. The same thing happened to me." He laughed but kept his eyes on Anderson's house.

"The same thing happened to you?" I was surprised. Shane looked like he could get a date in a convent. "Yeah, that happens to everybody."

"Well, what did you do when you saw her? Weren't you embarrassed?" I was more than interested.

Shane began playing with his moustache and paused before he continued. "Of course, I was embarrassed. Well, my dad gave me some good advice. He told me about the 'watch theory.'"

"The watch theory?" I sipped on my coffee, hoping to hear one of the secrets of the universe.

"He said, 'Shane, the next time you see that girl, you start talking to her, like real polite and interested. Then stop, look at your watch, and say real polite, 'Gee, I'd love to keep talking to you but I gotta get going.' You'll walk away and she'll stand there. She'll say to herself, 'Hey, I thought he liked me.' It will start her thinking."

"Does it work?" I pleaded.

"It seems to."

"But, does it work on all girls?"

"Orville, you gotta understand something. The 'watch theory' isn't geared to just girls. It's not about girls. It's about relationships. It works on boys as well as girls." Shane laughed.

"What do you mean?"

"Who do you think my dad learned the 'watch theory' from?"

"I don't know?"

"My Mom did it to him when he wasn't interested in her. My Dad said when she looked at her watch and then said she had to get going it sent the message that she didn't have time for him. That made him think, 'Hey, why isn't she interested in me?' Then he was determined to get to know her better. Little did they know it would lead to marriage." We both began laughing. Shane was like the big brother I never had.

We watched Anderson's doorway and didn't say anything for the next two hours. At 10:30 PM, Anderson opened the side door and walked to his car. Shane gave me a quick glance and said under his breath, "This could be it!" I agreed, because all the other nights the latest Anderson had gone out was 9:30 PM, and that was for milk at the 7-Eleven. Something told me he wasn't thirsty for milk and cookies. He was up to something. He was wearing black jeans and a dark-colored button-down shirt. He got into his green

BMW and pulled out of his driveway.

Shane waited until Anderson was about fifty yards ahead of us before he fired up the van, and then waited about a minute more before he turned on his headlights. As Anderson drove in the direction of Mrs. Lyons's house, my palms became clammy and I began rocking back and forth in the passenger's seat. This is it, I thought, as we approached my street, Beach View Road. But Anderson passed Mrs. Lyons's and kept going. I looked over at Shane and he cautioned, "Don't worry, he just may be making sure she is asleep."

The BMW then pulled into Main Street and passed Lucy's Salon Shop, Bill's Donuts, and the Conference Table Restaurant, until it finally pulled into the parking lot of the Belltown Supermarket. We hung back as Anderson got out of his car and headed into the store.

"I can't believe I got all psyched to catch this guy, and he's going food shopping!" I said in disgust.

Shane ignored me and turned off the engine. I could tell by the look on his face that he had something on his mind.

"Orville, you stay here. I'll be right back." He opened the door.

"Where are you going?"

"To see if shopping is what Anderson is planning on doing."

"What if he sees you?"

"Enough with the questions, Orville. He won't see me!" Shane slammed the door. I realized I was probably beginning to annoy him with all my questions. It probably appeared to him that I was questioning his professional-ism. I wasn't. I just didn't understand what else Anderson would be doing in the supermarket other than shopping. As I waited for Shane, a blue Toyota hatchback passed me and drove behind the market. A half-minute later, Shane jogged over to the van and jumped in. He started the en-gine and answered my questions before I could ask them.

"Just as I thought. Anderson is setting up his alibi in case he ever gets questioned." Shane was breathing heavily.

"What do you mean?"

"I mean I was watching for a couple of seconds, and he was just throwing anything into the cart. He's going to sneak out and then sneak back in somehow without be-ing detected by anyone."

"Isn't that a shaky alibi—to go shopping at ten-thirty at night?"

"No, it's Labor Day weekend. He could say he just wanted to pick up a few groceries."

I knew he didn't want any more questions, and I wasn't going to push it.

"I wonder, how he's going to leave?" Shane said.

"Oh, my God!" I screamed.

"What, Orville?"

"When you were inside I saw a blue Toyota hatch-back drive around to the back of the store!"

Shane didn't say a word. In one motion he put the van in drive and raced behind the building. As we made the turn to the back of the building, we spotted the tail-lights of the hatchback heading for the dirt road behind the Belltown Supermarket.

There were two people in the car. That must be the guy Maria heard Anderson talking to on the phone, I thought. Shane gave them extra room to breathe because the road we were on was not a well-traveled road. We followed without lights for the same reason. The hatchback bumped along slowly down the dusty road until it came to the end, where it connected onto Main Street. Shane picked up speed as the hatchback headed toward the beach. We weren't positive Anderson was in the car, but we both had a gut feeling going. At the top of Beach View Road, the hatchback came to an abrupt stop, and a man hopped out of the passenger side. Shane turned into a driveway and slammed on the brakes. We both slid down on our seats when the hatchback made a U-turn and headed past us. Shane threw it into reverse, and we turned back onto the street. Mrs. Lyons's house was another hundred yards up the street. There was no sign of the guy who had gotten out of the passenger side. Shane drove another fifty yards and put the car in park.

"OK, Orville, this is it!" Shane gave a loud whisper. I just nodded.

"I want to catch him in the act. You stay here! Keep your eyes out for his ride! If he comes back before I nab Anderson, call for help. All right?" Shane slapped for his gun.

"OK."

Shane shut the door softly and slipped up the street and into the camouflage of the night. My teeth rattled. This was definitely it! I was scared. I was also helpless. All I could do was wait. The night was like a dark movie screen, and I knew it would soon be filled with action! I just wished I could do something! My thoughts were blinded by headlights that lit up the night. It was the hatchback! It parked twenty yards in front of me.

"Oh, my God! Oh, my God!"

I slid lower into my seat. The man got out of the car, casually took out a match, and began lighting a cigarette. The match's light lit up his face.

"Oh, my God!" I screeched. His face was just lit up enough for me to be able to recognize it. I had seen that face a thousand times—Sergeant Gonestone.

"Oh, my God! Oh, my God! What am I gonna do?" I shook myself. I knew I couldn't call for backup. He probably had a police radio and would hear it. Worse than that, what if he had some dirty cops working for him!

"Oh, my God!" I kept saying, and shaking.

Gonestone suddenly turned and looked over in my direction. It was almost as if he'd sensed the van. I slid down deeper in my seat, but I could still see him. He turned sharply towards Mrs. Lyons's, as if he had heard something and then back towards the van and put it all together. He opened his car door. He was about to jump in when Anderson came running out of the darkness, yelling and pointing behind him. Gonestone put his hand up as if to say, "Don't worry!" Anderson dove into the passenger side of the Toyota. I was shivering. I figured Gonestone would jump in, too, but he didn't.

Gonestone drew his gun and pointed into the darkness. He was waiting for Shane! Shane was going to be ambushed, and there was nothing I could do! I snapped my head and saw that Shane had left the keys in the ignition! Of course! Shane had left the car idling. I ripped the gearshift down and put it in drive and then floored it. I could see Gonestone pointing his gun, and then I saw himturn around and point it at me . . . Then I saw nothing.

I woke up, not knowing what was going on. I began screaming, "Watch out, Shane! Watch out!" Shane pulled me out of the van, and hugged me.

"It's OK, Orville. You just passed out for a little bit when you hit their car." Shane was all smiles.

"What happened?" I had no idea.

Red-and-white and blue-and-white lights were coloring the night.

"What happened? You saved my life, buddy. Gonestone was shooting at me. He was gonna kill me, and then you plowed into their car. You saved my life!" He just kept smiling, and it was all coming back to me.

"Is he dead?" I managed.

"No. They'll both be in great shape for prison."

"Well, what happened to you and Anderson?"

"Mrs. Lyons heard all the noise and delayed me with a vase over my head." He laughed. We both laughed. Tears began flowing from my eyes. I don't know if they were tears of joy or relief or what, but they felt good!

The next day, all Belltown was buzzing about Anderson and Gonestone. Shane and I were being treated like heroes. I have to admit, it felt pretty good. A search through Anderson's office found all the evidence that would be needed to put him and Gonestone away for a long time. The only people who were not too pleased were my parents. Yes, they were proud of me, but as more and more information came out about my investigation, they were concerned about the danger I had put myself in. After all, they were my parents.

There was an emotion that was going through me that I just couldn't explain. I was both happy and sad that I had been right. The biggest surprise to me was that Gonestone had been involved. I really thought he was a law officer who just didn't know the law. I was wrong. He just didn't want to follow the law. By mid-afternoon, I could've opened a bakery—there were so many cakes and pastries delivered to our house, as a way of saying thanks. One was a coconut-cream pie with a note attached, "Thank you for believing." It was signed "Walter and Martha." That note meant so much to me, and I realize then why people want to become detectives.

That night Shane picked me up to give me a ride up the street to the beach. There was a huge beach party and bonfire planned as an end-of-the-summer sendoff. As we approached the beach, Shane handed me the tape recorder.

"In the closet?" I asked.

"Yes. Thank God it wasn't winter," Shane said.

"Why's that?"

"'Cause it fell behind his winter boots!" Shane laughed.

"Y'know, Orville, you're a pretty good detective."

"Thanks." I smiled.

"There's one thing I kept wanting to ask you."

"What's that, Shane?"

"Well, you felt that you couldn't trust anyone—even the police—and in this case, you were right. But what made you come to me? How could you know you could trust me?"

Shane squinted as he pulled up to the beach.

"A friend sent me."

"Who?" Shane questioned.

"His name is Will." I wasn't sure if Will wanted me to mention his name, but with all that had happened, I thought he should get some credit.

"Oh, man! Will! Will Michaels?"

"I don't know. Maybe."

"Yup, that's who it is." He shook his head.

"How do you know him?" I asked.

"He only jumped in front of a bullet meant for my dad's back. He's a good man. It's too bad what happened to him."

"Yeah, but he's getting better." I nodded.

"Will you tell him Russie's son says thanks?"

"Definitely." I got out of the car and shook Shane's hand.

"Until the next case, Shane." I laughed.

"Why is it that I think that's not just a joke?" He gave me a smirk.

I tilted my head sideways, smiled, and shrugged. He knew it was in my blood!

The only time we were allowed to have a bonfire on the beach was the last day of summer. The smell of sea and smoke told me summer was over, and Mr. Reason's math class was around the corner. I was going to savor every last flame, and it looked like Joe Clancy was going to savor every last marshmallow. His Luke Skywalker shirt had taken quite a beating and the dripping marshmallows were something of a grand finale for him. Everyone sat around the fire and listened to my tale. When I was done, Mark approached me and apologized for losing touch, and not making good on his pact to visit Will. I accepted his apology, and apologized to him also for being a jerk. Perhaps we were both thinking of Maria. Mark let her monopolize his time. I let her monopolize my mind.

As I began walking down the boardwalk for home, Maria came up to me.

"Orville, we didn't talk all night," she said.

"Is that a fact?" I said.

"Yeah, I thought, y'know we could go for a walk and talk."

"Oh, OK."

We began walking along the beach. Maria was chattering away, and we kept bumping into each other as our feet sank in the sand. I was dying to try the 'watch theory,' and I played the whole scene over in my mind. Suddenly Maria stopped and looked at her watch.

"Geez, look at the time," she said "You know," she said politely, "I'd love to go on, but I really have to get back."

I giggled. Then I laughed like a crazy man. Did Maria know the 'watch theory?' I wondered. Maybe down the road I would have a chance with my dream girl. She looked at me, puzzled at my laughter, and then walked off. "Well, good job, Orville!" she half-yelled back at me.

Orville, I thought. My name is Orville Jacques. What a

stupid name! Do you think I'd change it? No way! I was beginning to like it. It was different. I looked down at my watch and realized I had about two hours before I had to get home. I knew what I had to do. I had to learn how to play horseshoes!

Look for all of the books in T. M. Murphy's Belltown Mystery Series:

Millbury Public Library

About the Author

T. M. MURPHY lives in Falmouth, Massachusetts. When he is not writing or cheering for the Boston Red Sox, Mr. Murphy enjoys teaching creative writing to young people. He lives and teaches his Just Write It class in a converted garage he calls The Shack.

Photo by Amy Hamilton

Millbury Public Library

9/02

Millbury Public Library